D0768977

Evil in the 1st House

Books by Mitchell Scott Lewis

The Starlight Detective Agency Mysteries
Murder in the 11th House
Death in the 12th House: Where Neptune Rules
Evil in the 1st House

Evil in the 1st House

A Starlight Detective Agency Mystery

Mitchell Scott Lewis

Poisoned Pen Press

Copyright © 2014 by Mitchell Scott Lewis

First Edition 2014

10 9 8 7 6 5 4 3 2 1

Library of Congress Catalog Card Number: 2013933214

ISBN: 9781464201875   Hardcover
       9781464201899   Trade Paperback

Poisoned Pen Press
6962 E. First Ave., Ste. 103
Scottsdale, AZ 85251
www.poisonedpenpress.com
info@poisonedpenpress.com

Printed in the United States of America

This book is dedicated to my students
And to all who seek the truth

Acknowledgments

My deepest thanks for your help and support:

Sandra Bond, Annette Rogers, Jessica Tribble, Barbara Peters, Rob Rosenwald, everyone at Poisoned Pen Press, Carl Lennertz, Fiona Druckenmiller, Roberta Cary, Yale Cohen, David Lewis, Sidney Lewis, Ray Blumenfeld, Audrey Blumenfeld, and Goldie Lewis.

The planets are always aligned.
It is we who are askew.

—David Lowell

Chapter One

"He says it's a matter of life and death," Sarah whispered urgently over the intercom.

Before Lowell could answer, a tall, well-dressed man carrying a brown, leather briefcase pushed open the office door and strode to the desk. He carried himself with an air of self-importance as he dropped the briefcase on the floor and placed a card in front of the detective.

"Mr. Williamson," Sarah introduced from behind, raising her eyebrows as she closed the door.

David Lowell, being a creature of habit, preferred to conduct his morning in a particular order and did not like his routine upset.

"I'm extremely busy and can't accept another client."

"Perhaps once you've heard my story."

Lowell looked down at the business card in front of him. "Mr. Williamson, I can spare you exactly five minutes." The notoriety of the recent rock 'n' roll murder case had increased demands and stretched Lowell's limits of both time and patience.

"Thank you sir, I appreciate it. Actually, it's *Doctor* Edgar Williamson. I don't put it on the card, as I'm primarily in research these days, not a practicing physician." He sat in one of the two leather client's chairs. "Let me be clear. I appreciate your time and your talents, and I have a vital need for both. I understand you're rich. Please forgive my bluntness, but as time is at a premium I have no choice."

Impatient but intrigued, Lowell tugged at his salt and pepper ponytail.

"So I'm sure money won't be sufficient motivation. Still…" Williamson reached down and picked up the briefcase, placed it on the desk facing Lowell, and opened it. The case was filled with crisp, neatly bound, one hundred-dollar bills. "That's a million dollars. And it's yours up front if you will take my case, whether you are successful or not."

Lowell took a fleeting look at the cash. "Now what could be important enough to risk that kind of money?"

"The only thing in the world that matters to me. My son Edward. Money is the least of my worries."

"I'll listen to your story. But if you'll just wait a moment, I'd like my associate, Mort, to come in."

He pushed a button on the intercom and several moments later the door opened and a man with limbs too long for his body entered the room. He walked with a quirky, erratic gait.

"Mort, this is Dr. Williamson. He's interested in hiring us and was just about to tell me his story. I'd like you to hear it as well."

"How do you do?" Mort nodded as he sat in the second client's chair. When he saw the cash-filled briefcase he and Lowell exchanged a momentary look. Mort could see Lowell was hooked.

Williamson sat forward. "My son, Edward, is fifteen years old and the most important thing in my life. His mother and I had a contentious separation soon after he was born and she left, taking Edward's twin brother, Kevin. I've devoted much of my life to raising my boy. I've been very fortunate financially and want for nothing material. But Edward has advanced kidney disease, and without a transplant I don't believe he will last much longer. I would give every penny I have to keep him alive."

"And how can we be of help?" asked Lowell.

"His blood type is quite rare, something he inherits from my side of the family, and we haven't been able to find a donor match. The most difficult part of a transplant is the body's tendency to reject the new organ and the antigens that form the human leukocyte antigen, or HLA system. But because

Edward is an identical twin his DNA is indistinguishable from his brother's. His body would not reject the kidney. It would recognize the new organ as if it were his own."

"You have our full attention. Please." Lowell waved his arm.

"I'm a surgeon by trade, and have performed countless transplant operations in my career. I'm a firm believer in the donor program. Without organ donors many people would be denied the opportunity to continue a fruitful life. I've signed on as a potential donor myself. One of my kidneys was damaged in an accident years ago or I'd give Edward one of mine."

He crossed his legs, straightening the crease in his pants. "My son has little time. I've been unable to find Kevin. I've hired the most expensive detective agencies in the world, and they haven't come up with anything. Until now. A detective in California, where I thought they were living, got a lead that suggested Kevin and his mother may be somewhere in the northeast. I need someone who knows the turf."

"And you would like us to find your son's twin?"

"It's the only way to save his life. And time is short."

"Have you contacted the police?"

"No." His tone was adamant. "No police. This is a private matter. If my story were to become public knowledge I would be at the mercy of every con artist on the planet. I'm relying on your discretion in this matter."

"You're familiar with my methods?"

"Yes. I understand that you use astrology in your work."

"Much more than that. Astrology is the very foundation of my practice."

"I have little knowledge of it one way or the other, but I pride myself on being open-minded. Your reputation precedes you and frankly, I'm in no position to question your methods. Time is not on my side here."

Lowell turned to his computer. "May I have your sons' birth information?"

"They were born in Princeton, New Jersey, on June 10th, 1999. Kevin was born at 3:30 a.m. Edward followed at 3:44 a.m."

"Appropriate to arrive in Gemini, the sign of the twins," said Lowell. "Are you certain about the birth times?"

"I delivered them myself, so yes I'm quite positive."

"Dr. Williamson, your case is intriguing, and I'll look into it. But I will not take one million dollars if I fail to find your son."

"Then I insist that you hold it as collateral. You may return some amount if our relationship concludes unsatisfactorily."

Lowell smiled slightly. "I'll have Sarah write you a receipt for the money."

"That won't be necessary. I trust my judgment in people. Besides, what good would it do to chase you for the money, with or without a receipt?"

"Fine. May I ask how you accrued your wealth?"

"I hold several extremely valuable patents."

"Are you an inventor?"

"No, these are genetic patents."

"I see." Lowell nodded. "I'll need your wife's birth information: date, place, and time."

"I understand. I believe I have a copy of her birth certificate at home somewhere. I'll email it to you. I don't know if the time of birth is included. Is that important?"

"Yes. It may make the difference between being able to find them or not."

"Really? Okay."

"I also will need your birth information."

"Mine? What has that got to do with anything?"

"It may prove useful in finding your son. There's something called reflective astrology where we see others within someone's chart. I can look for your children and your marriage partner in your chart. Sometimes it's useful, sometimes not."

"Well, of course I know my birthday, but not the time. I'll check. I'm sure I have my birth certificate somewhere. I'll try to find it for you, though I don't know if the birth time is on it either."

"Just get me whatever you can."

The big man stood, throwing his shoulders back, intimidating in both size and manner. "I'll call you later with that information."

◇◇◇

Mort gazed out the window after Williamson left, allowing David time.

Lowell was silent for a few moments. Then he turned. "What did you think?"

Mort shifted in his chair. "I think it's a pretty weird story."

"So do I."

"But you might take the case?"

"Yes."

"Because it's weird enough?"

Lowell laughed. "Maybe."

Mort nodded thoughtfully. "I think there's a lot more to it than he's telling."

"What did you get from him?"

Mort was a master hacker who had been asked to leave MIT after using its computers to get into secret U.S. government sites. Rather than face the embarrassment of prosecuting him, the government, recognizing his unique ability to circumvent normal boundaries on the Internet, offered him a job hacking for them, which he turned down. He was also a psychic who could read the emotions and thoughts of those around him. Most of the time. Once Lowell realized that Mort could not read his, he hired him for his computer skills and his other abilities. Lowell paid attention to what Mort felt and had found his instincts right on the money most of the time.

"His anxiety was quite strong."

Lowell unknotted his ponytail and retied it. "Could you tell what scared him?"

"No. Only that the fear was strong and very real. And it felt very personal, as one would expect at the fear of losing a child."

"Okay, after I get his birth information and his wife's, I can understand it better. In the meantime find out what you can about Dr. Williamson and his estranged family. I need as much information as I can get if I'm going to find the boy in time."

Mort nodded.

Lowell hit the intercom. "Sarah, come in here, please."

The door opened. "What's up boss?" Sarah unconsciously pushed her bright red hair back behind her ears. She wore a dark blue collared sleeveless blouse, designer faded blue-jeans, pre-torn in spots to reveal just a bit of skin, with silver buttons running down the sides, and aqua shoes. Monochromatic shading from head to toe.

When she saw the cash-filled briefcase her eyes bulged. "What's that?"

"A million dollars in cash."

"Don't see that everyday."

Lowell took the briefcase and walked over to the wall opposite his desk and pushed a hidden button underneath a Modigliani print. A spring released, and the print slid sideways revealing a wall safe. He swiftly spun the dial and the safe opened, then he pushed a few folders aside to make room for the briefcase. Lowell rarely kept anything of monetary value in the safe, mostly paperwork. It was state of the art, and he relied on the safe to protect his most valuable possessions: notes from his cases, astrological charts of some very prominent people who might not be happy if their information became common knowledge, and a diary he had kept since his days trading on Wall Street.

"I just wanted you to be aware that the money's here in the safe. I've taken Dr. Williamson's case. It involves his missing son." Lowell looked at his two colleagues. "Now that we're getting busier, I'm going to need you both to be on top of things."

He handed out assignments and sent Mort and Sarah to their tasks.

Lowell closed the safe and walked to the window. The unobstructed view of the Empire State Building from his window was a source of great joy, and he never tired of seeing its majestic stance. He took a container of turtle food and sprinkled a bit near his two red-eared slider turtles.

"Hello, Buster," he said to the first, as she waddled over to the food. "Hello, Keaton," he greeted the other, as he too lumbered toward the goodies.

When he'd opened the Starlight Detective Agency eight years before, they were the size of his thumb. Now they were each a foot long and growing. He watched them eat for a few moments, enjoying the morning ritual.

Chapter Two

The intercom buzzed. "Yes, Sarah?"

"Melinda's here."

"Send her in."

"There's also a woman on the other line from a cable station who wants you to do a reality show about astrology."

"There are hundreds of excellent astrologers who would love the opportunity to be on TV. If she calls back, suggest astrologers we have on file. Or have her call one of the astrology organizations, like the NCGR or AFAN."

"She's more interested in using your renown to help herself rather than help someone else."

"I think you're right."

"That's why you pay me the big bucks." She laughed. "Anything you need?"

"Order me breakfast from Louie's." Louie's was his favorite organic restaurant, run by an old hippie from Vermont who'd inherited the building several years before and moved his restaurant down to Manhattan. The menu had many selections that suited Lowell's vegetarian diet.

"What do you want?"

"Surprise me."

The door opened and an attractive brunette in an expensive business suit entered. She walked over to the desk and bent to kiss Lowell on his forehead. "Hi, Dad." At six feet she towered over Lowell's five-foot-eight frame.

He smiled and leaned back in his chair. "You look tired, Melinda."

"You tell me that every time I see you."

"That's because you look tired every time I see you. Why won't you let me set you up with your own law practice?"

"Why, so I can work a hundred hours a week instead of seventy? I'm only thirty-two. I'd like to try to have a life outside the office."

"Eventually you'll come to the same conclusion I have: it's better to work for yourself. Especially with your natal chart. What brings you around?"

"I have to see a client in the neighborhood, and I thought I'd come by and say hello."

"They overwork you terribly."

"Dad, I'm fine, really."

"Do you need any money?"

"No, thank you. I make a good living."

He nodded. "I spoke to your mother last night."

"I've been meaning to call her. How's she doing?"

"Hello Catherine."

"How are you, David?"

"Is there ever really a simple answer? I've been okay. A little tired. Getting very busy with my work."

His ex-wife sighed. "I've been reading about you. Freddie Finger's murder even made the Woodstock papers. How sad. Remember the first time we saw him in concert?"

He chuckled. "How could I forget? You wore yellow shoes and a very short blue dress. You never wore dresses in those days. Always jeans. And sneakers with no laces. Once I saw that dress I knew we were going to finally get together as a couple that night."

"Sure of yourself, weren't you?"

"Not until I saw that dress."

She laughed. "I must have tried on thirty outfits before my roommate lent me that one."

"She must have been pissed when you returned it full of grass stains after our rendezvous under the stars."

They both laughed.

Then there was silence.

"Is there something on your mind, David?"

He sipped his beer and gazed out the window of his Manhattan townhouse at the tiny piece of backyard property fenced in on three sides with high wooden panels. He wasn't feeling well, and he couldn't put his finger on it until now when his eyes fell upon that urban oasis enclosed like a child's dollhouse. He felt claustrophobic. His life seemed to be closing in around him, like that wooden fence.

When he heard ice clink in a glass, he knew she was drinking Sauvignon blanc. She drank it with ice in the summer.

"I was thinking of taking a drive later in the week," he said, "and was wondering if you'd like some company. I haven't been up to Woodstock in a while and would like to come up to visit. I miss…the house."

"Is Melinda alright?"

"Yes, our daughter's fine."

"Thank God." She sipped her wine. "I suppose if your mind is set on it there's little I can do to dissuade you."

"It's going to be a beautiful weekend," he said quietly, "and I thought it would be nice to take a walk and have dinner. I love that old farmhouse restaurant in town."

"Okay, David. Next Saturday?"

"I'll have Andy drive me up in the early afternoon. I'll see if Melinda would like to join us."

"It would be nice to spend some time together."

"I'll call you on the way."

When they hung up, Lowell went out to the backyard and sat for almost an hour, beer forgotten in hand, staring at the fence.

"Dad?"

"Oh, sorry. She sounded okay. I'm driving up next weekend, and I was wondering if you'd like to come along."

Melinda walked over to the window and picked up the turtle's food. She sprinkled a little into the tank and watched as Buster and Keaton shambled over for a second treat. "It's that time of year again, isn't it?"

Lowell was silent.

"Yes, I guess I'll come up." She gazed out the window. "It doesn't get any easier with time, does it?"

"Not really. But it would be good to get together as a family."

"I miss him everyday."

"So do I."

Melinda nodded. "Okay, when do you want to leave?"

"Saturday morning about nine."

"Will Andy pick me up, or should I come up to the town-house?"

"Andy will get you. Unless you want to stay over Friday night."

"I'll check my social calendar and let you know." Melinda had made finger quotes when referring to her social life. "What are you working on?"

"There are a few things I'm looking into. I just took a rather unusual case."

She laughed. "You don't get any other kind. What is it?"

"A Dr. Williamson asked me to find his son's identical twin. According to him they were separated shortly after birth when the wife apparently took off with one of the children. The boy has advanced kidney disease and needs a transplant which, because of a rare blood type, apparently only his missing twin brother can supply."

Melinda turned from the window and looked at her father. "Not your usual case. Do you have the charts yet?"

Lowell shook his head. "Only for the boys."

"Why did the wife run off? And why did she only take one son?"

"I don't know. There are a lot of things about this situation that seem a little weird. I have to wait for the parents' birth information before I can really move forward. Williamson was oddly reluctant to supply his own details on the spot. I let it go for now until I figure this guy out."

"Why wouldn't he tell you?"

Lowell shrugged. "He's supposed to email me his and his wife's birth information. I need to find out a lot more about the parents if I'm going to find the child."

"Sounds like it's time for a Mort special."

Lowell nodded. "Best Internet guy I've ever known. Whatever data's out there about this guy, Mort will find it." He turned to the computer screen. "Let's look at the twins' charts."

Melinda was his best astrology student.

Having already put the information into his Solar Fire computer program, Lowell brought the two charts up simultaneously on his computer screen then hit a button which directed the image to the 32-inch flat screen TV against the wall.

"Here are the two charts. They were born on June 10th, 1999 at 3:30 a.m. and 3:44 a.m. in Princeton, New Jersey. Edward, the younger of the two, is the one who's ill. What do you see?"

Melinda pulled her chair closer to the desk. She took the wireless mouse in hand and used it as a pointer. "Hmm. As you taught me, Venus rules the kidneys, so let's see how it's aspected in the natal chart." She gazed at the screen moving the pointer as she spoke. "The ascendant is Taurus, ruled by Venus, so that planet will have a big influence on the boys."

He leaned back in his chair and brushed a piece of lint off his jeans. "Right. And how is Venus aspected?" He couldn't help taking on the professor role.

"It's badly afflicted. Venus is in opposition to Neptune," she wiggled the mouse back and forth between the two planets, "a very weakening aspect. It shows the potential for infections, breakdowns, and possibly misdiagnosed ailments in the kidneys and water meridian."

Lowell smiled proudly. "What else? Why is one boy ill and the other not? What's different about their charts?"

She looked for a few moments and then smiled. "The Moon. Both boys have the Moon in the 12th house that rules medicine and hospitals. But the older boy, Kevin has the Moon at twenty-nine degrees fifty-two minutes of Aries. Because of the fourteen minutes' difference in the births, Edward has the Moon at zero degrees Taurus, which adds to the Venus influence. That's a major difference, isn't it? The Taurus Moon in Edward's chart is also in a close square to Venus and Neptune, both at four degrees, creating a tight in-sign t-square resolving in the 6th house of health, which in this chart is also ruled by Venus."

Lowell nodded. "Right. Just about what I would expect with kidney failure at such a young age. As you know, I've always been a strong believer in sign placement, not just the degrees of an aspect. The Moon has a lot to do with the immune system as well. And because Edward's Moon squares Venus, it implies that he could have health issues involving the kidneys and the immune system, which may not afflict his brother. Anything else different between the two horoscopes that could affect their health?"

Melinda moved the pointer. "The different birth time also moves the ascendant six degrees, giving Kevin a twelve-degree rising sign, and making Edward's eighteen degrees. The change puts Kevin's Saturn in the first house of the self. He may act more maturely than his brother, and could look older as they age. Edward's birth time creates a different ascendant and puts Saturn, the planet of restriction and limitations, in the 12th house of hospitals. The indication is that there is the possibility that, at some point in his life, Edward could be forced to stay in a hospital or other institution."

"Excellent."

"So what I understand about twins, if the problem isn't genetic, it's environmental, particularly how the children developed in the womb. That's why only one identical twin may become sickly."

"But it should still show up in the natal charts."

"And what about fate?"

"It has to do with what each person needs to experience in this life. One soul may need to learn to suffer physically in order to rebalance his karmic bank account, while the other must learn patience and unconditional love for the sibling. They come back as twins, one ill, the other not, so they can work through their necessary lessons. Just being twins shows the remarkable con-nection between the souls. Something that goes back beyond the time of conception."

"Fascinating!" She looked at her watch. "Dad, I'm so sorry. I've got to go. But I'm interested in this case. Keep me up to date. I'll talk to you before Saturday." She stood up.

Lowell pushed his chair back away from the desk. "Oh, there is one more little detail I should mention."

"What's that?"

"Dr. Williamson gave me a briefcase with a million dollars in hundred-dollar bills as a retainer."

"This definitely ups the 'unusual' quotient."

Chapter Three

As always, David Lowell awoke at five. He showered and dressed in his usual blue jeans pressed to a sharp crease, a lightweight turtleneck, gray today, and loafers. Then he left his townhouse on East Ninety-third Street and walked down to his offices on East Twenty-fourth as was his habit since he opened the Starlight Detective Agency almost eight years before. This was the only time of the day he could call his own. No clients screaming for his attention, no traumas or distractions. It was a meditative ritual that allowed him to clear his head and prepare for the day's action. He stopped at a Starbucks to pick up his first cup of the day and strolled leisurely downtown.

Each day he took a different route. This time he walked down Museum Mile: the Guggenheim, in its circular glory, Frank Lloyd Wright's twisted amusement park of visual delights. Then he passed the magnificent Met, the largest art museum in America, its stately, imposing steps leading to one of the greatest collections of human endeavors. With its Beaux-Arts façade a quarter of a mile long, and covering almost two million square feet, it beckoned with creative works from all corners of the globe.

He passed the mansions of the Gilded Age, each a square block and once the private homes of the robber barons of the Nineteenth century, now mostly all museums.

At Seventieth Street he came upon the Frick Museum, built in 1914 as a private mansion by Henry Clay Frick, the chairman

of the Carnegie Steel Company, during a time when such out-
rageous opulence by the elite was the order of the day. High
wrought-iron fences protecting its glorious gardens complete
with marble benches scattered along a winding path that invoked
a fading memory of a smaller, gentler New York City. Now it
stood as a stark reminder of those heady days, and evidence of
a way of life long past, yet still somehow relevant as an aide-
memoir in the Twenty-first century. After all, how different are
they from the grand estates built by the robber barons of the
Internet Age? Perhaps in time they will all be museums, too.

He crossed the avenue and meandered along the stone wall
bordering Central Park. At its southern end at Fifty-ninth Street
he turned east and headed over to Lexington where he continued
downtown. He enjoyed walking through midtown before it
awakened for the day, and before the summer sun got too hot.
The building supers were out hosing the sidewalks down, and
the cold water on the warm cement created welcome pockets
of cool air.

I Ie passed Grand Central Station, a massive endeavor when
built, now dwarfed by the ever-growing city, ghostly in its
silence, soon to be inundated with harried commuters. Its ceiling,
painted by artists Paul Helleu and Charles Basing, included a
complete display of the zodiac that always made Lowell chuckle
when he walked through its giant corridor. The sky is painted
backwards. Nobody seems to know if it was a mistake or if
reversing the heavens had some hidden meaning for the artists.

He ambled through Murray Hill in the east Thirties and into
Little India, passing dozens of restaurants already preparing for
the day's business, the pungent smell of curry seeping out of
windows and vents.

When Lowell reached Twenty-fourth Street he turned east
for two blocks, went into Starbucks on the corner and picked up
his second coffee of the day. Retracing his steps for a quarter of
a block, he entered a nondescript brown building, and took the
elevator to the sixth floor, opened the office door, and entered the
suite of the Starlight Detective Agency. The inner office housed

his familiar work space and occasional home-away-from-home. He picked up the phone and pushed #7 on the speed dial.

"Smith Barney."

"Roger Bowman, please."

"One moment."

"This is Roger."

"It's David."

"Hey, Starman. Nice job on the rock 'n' roll murder case. I hear everyone was talking about it in the oil pit. What's up today?'

"I'm going long on the metals again. Buy twenty silver market-on-open and ten gold, also on-the-open. Put the stop in silver at 19.75, and the gold at 1360."

"Sure, I'll call you with the fills."

"How did we do this month?"

"Your accounts are up about four percent."

"Good. Please send half of the profits to the ASPCA."

"Will do. Coming down anytime soon? You're famous now. And the Freedom Tower at Battery Park City is almost completed. You should see it."

"I'll let you know."

Sarah buzzed him twice to announce her arrival. He returned the buzz. It was nine a.m. on the dot.

Sarah picked up. "What's up, Boss?"

"Did Williamson ever email the birth information I requested?"

"Not yet."

"Call him and remind him."

About five minutes later Sarah buzzed. "Machine picked up. I left a message."

"Let me know if you hear from him. When Mort comes in send him in here."

"He's just coming in the front door."

A few moments later Mort appeared, coffee cup in one hand, a strawberry Danish in the other. "Morning, David. What's up?" He took a bite, then a sip.

"Mort, I can't wait any longer. Find the birth information for Williamson and his wife. He's delinquent in sending it, and I need it before I can proceed."

"I'll get right on it."

An hour later Mort knocked twice on Lowell's door.

Lowell looked up from his computer. "Mort, what did you find out?"

"Here's Williamson's birth date and place. I haven't got the birth time yet." He handed Lowell a piece of paper. "You know, it wasn't as easy to find as you might expect for such a prominent person in his field. It's almost as if he went to some lengths to hide it. He just didn't do such a great job." Mort beamed that big goofy grin of his.

"How?"

"Well, there are a number of profiles of him as a young doctor, but none mention his place or date of birth. It's not even on Wikipedia. I find that most unusual."

"So how did you find it?"

"I worked backwards until I hit a crossroads in his college days. I was able to hack into Columbia's database and then back to his high school, etc. I actually got confirmation of the birth date through his pediatrician's records when he was a child. The practice was taken over by the doctor's son who for some reason put all the old files online. I've got to go out to the hospital in New Brunswick where Williamson was born later today to get into their old records for the birth time."

Lowell looked at him with real admiration. "You continue to amaze me. Andy will drive you out there when you're ready."

"Well, as you like to say, you didn't hire me for my looks." He laughed loudly. "Okay, here's what else I found that I thought you'd find interesting. Early in his career Williamson was a superstar. A surgeon with an almost perfect record and a keen intuition. But then sometime before his marriage he began to change. His interest morphed into making as much money as possible. He got into the business of genetic patents and accrued a large number of them, some apparently through less-than-ethical means."

"What do you mean?"

"He was sued by one woman with a very rare genetic marker in her blood capable of fighting off certain cancer cells. She'd come to him for some blood work, and he patented her blood type using some discarded samples. It's all been perfectly legal, although it's becoming more of a gray area since the recent Supreme Court ruling implying that many DNA patents may be illegal."

"What happened with the lawsuit?"

"Nothing. The woman died in a hit-and-run accident before it came to court, and the case was dropped."

"So Williamson became more concerned with gene patents than with practicing medicine?"

Mort waved his arms erratically as he spoke. "Apparently. He does own quite a number of them. He has laid claim to about forty genome abnormalities."

"Is this common?"

"The purchasing, or in some cases, stealing of genes has been an escalating business for some years. He owns some that are essential for diabetics, people with Parkinson's, and several other high profile diseases. His patents are used by the biggest drug companies in the world. And they pay him a percentage of everything they earn on any drug that uses one of them. I'll bet he's even richer than you." Mort smiled broadly.

"What else do you have?"

"I'm still chasing down some leads."

Lowell took the last sip from his tall cardboard cup of coffee, then crumpled it and tossed it overhand like a basketball into the recycle bin. He looked at the paper Mort had given him. "I'll get to Williamson's chart later, once you find out the birth time. Anything else?"

Mort glanced at his notes. "He was married to Gloria Greenwald in New Jersey in 1998. There is no record of a divorce in New York or New Jersey. But they could have done it in Reno. I'll keep looking."

"Birth information for her?"

"Not yet. But later today."

"And after the separation?"

"He seems to have thrown himself into his work. No record of a new marriage. Edward wanted for nothing. He went to the finest schools and traveled around the world. He even spent one semester in a boarding school in Paris."

Lowell nodded knowingly. He understood the extent of elite education in a moneyed life. "Where is his son now?"

"Williamson owns a small, private hospital outside Clifton, New Jersey, which is where the boy is being treated. There are only eight rooms on the second floor. It appears to be mostly a research hospital."

"Alright, we'll look into that later. For now, I need the mother's birth information if I'm ever going to find her."

"I'll get right on it. I'll work on the computer in the limo on the way to New Brunswick and kill two birds with one stone."

"When can you leave?"

Mort looked at his phone. "It's almost ten now. I can be ready by eleven."

Lowell buzzed Sarah. "Have Andy pick Mort up outside at eleven."

Mort got up to leave and then turned, his hand resting on the doorknob. "You know, David, something's just not right here."

"I know. I feel it too." Lowell stood up and stretched his back, then sat down again. "Let's use our respective skills to get to the truth."

Chapter Four

Waiting was the hardest thing for Lowell to do. Once he had a lead he could follow it like a bloodhound tracking a coyote. But now he felt stuck on the front porch waiting for Mort's information.

But he was also working on a case involving the embezzlement of a company's retirement fund. With the twins' inquiry on hold, he took out that folder and looked it over.

It was a particularly nasty business. Someone had absconded with the retirement money that sixty-three people relied on. He carried the charts of the three main suspects over to the turtle tank. Buster perched on the rock waiting for him. She always was more interested in his astrological discussions than Keaton. He began reading the charts out loud.

"It's called The Happy Snappy Marshmallow Company, but I don't see anything happy about it. Most of these people have worked their entire lives for this company, putting away a little at a time for decades to ensure a decent old age. Now the money is gone. Even if I can identify the culprit and we can prove culpability, there's a chance they may never get the money back if it has been hidden or moved offshore. Time is more of an issue here than I first realized."

He shuffled through the charts. "According to the president of the company, three main suspects had access to the accounts. Each has an afflicted chart in some ways." He held out one paper to the turtle. "Here is the bookkeeper's chart. The ruler of her 2nd house of money and values is in opposition to Neptune, the most confusing and unreliable planet. She has never had a clear sense of reality when it comes to what's important, and she may have a gambling problem or some other spending issues. Her attitude toward money and possessions is convoluted and she is very capable of deception."

Buster's gaze remained fixed on Lowell as he spoke.

He turned to the next chart. "This is the vice-president's horoscope. He has a Moon-Pluto square and Mars conjunct Saturn, both difficult and unsociable aspects. While I wouldn't want to be friends with this person, I don't think it's the chart of a thief. What do you think?"

Buster seemed to shrug and shake her head.

"I agree. I don't think it was the vice-president either." He raised another chart. "Here's the third suspect, a junior partner with access to the accounts as well. Also an afflicted chart with Neptune in square to the Sun and Mars. He lacks self-confidence and can often be confused. But he doesn't have the ego or willpower to accomplish a theft of this magnitude. How this company ever lasted so long with this mishmash of neurotics is a mystery."

He wrote a few notes on each chart, and then announced his decision. "It's the bookkeeper."

Buster nodded, albeit slowly.

"Good." He slipped the charts back in the folder and sat. "Now all we have to do is prove it."

Buster didn't move. She was a more effective consultant than investigator.

He hit the intercom button. "Sarah, get me Buddy Ferguson at The Happy Snappy Marshmallow Company."

She giggled. "Sorry, Boss, the name just cracks me up."

"Well, try to contain your amusement."

In a moment his phone rang. "Mr. Ferguson?"

"Buddy, please. Everyone calls me Buddy."

"Okay, Buddy. I believe I've narrowed down the suspects to one. But now it's a matter of proof and finding the money before it disappears, if it's not already too late."

"Who is it?"

"Your bookkeeper."

Buddy let out a long exhale. "Oh no, not Harriet. She's been with me for more than a decade. Couldn't be. Are you certain?"

"Pretty much," said Lowell. "And she's probably been planning this for some time. Is she still working for you?"

"Oh, yes. She comes in most days exactly on time. Although she occasionally works from home." Buddy took a deep breath. "How can you know for sure? You haven't even met her."

"This is what I do. I often interpret the charts of people I never meet. I don't think she was working alone. This is too much money to move. She must have someone in a bank or other financial institution who could handle that large a transaction without creating suspicion. The ruler of her 3rd house of siblings and relatives is heavily aspected, which means there may be a family member directly involved in this affair. Is there someone in her family in a position to move this kind of money?"

"Her brother is the vice-president of a regional bank in Georgia."

Lowell nodded to himself. "That's where you'll find the trail. Act quickly or the money will be transferred offshore. I suspect that her brother will give notice, and they both will disappear forever. What's the brother's name, and what bank does he work for?"

"Southeastern Mutual. His name is John Collins."

Lowell wrote down the information. He'd have Mort find the brother's birth date and then look at the charts anew.

Buddy was upset, though his voice kept its melodic lilt. "I'm going to confront her right now."

Lowell tugged on his ponytail. "I wouldn't do that if I were you. You'll alert her to your suspicions and force her to move more quickly. Instead, contact the FBI. Let them know what's going on and ask for an audit on the bank."

"We don't want this made public. Our company is a family business with a squeaky clean image to uphold. Publicity would be a disaster."

"More so than your retirees losing their pensions?"

Buddy clicked his tongue against his teeth. "Damn it. No, I suppose not. Okay, I'll contact the Feds. You'll stay on top of it too, won't you?"

"Yes," said Lowell, "until the money is either recovered or obviously lost. My associates and I will follow up on leads and do what we can to help."

After Lowell hung up, he looked at the bookkeeper's chart again. He was quite sure she was the one. The 3rd house of siblings was ruled by an afflicted Jupiter in her chart showing the lack of restraint or boundaries in her sibling. The brother's chart would tell him more.

◇◇◇

At about three in the afternoon, Sarah buzzed. "Mort's on line two and he sounds excited."

Lowell picked up the phone and Mort started right in. "We're just leaving the hospital in New Brunswick. You might need this info ASAP. Found a sympathetic worker in the records department and she made me a copy of Williamson's original birth certificate."

"Good work. How did you manage it?"

Mort chuckled. "I said I worked for an insurance company and had a large check to deliver, and needed proof of Williamson's birth. The woman was suspicious at first, but when I told her there was a hundred-dollar cash reward for any information, she was most helpful."

Lowell smiled. "So what have you got?"

"Born March 4th, 1965, confirming the date I gave you."

"Time?"

"10:03 a.m. eastern standard time."

"Where are you now?"

"We're heading back to the office. At the moment we're on the Jersey Turnpike and it looks like we'll get stuck at the entrance to the Holland Tunnel. But I'll crank up the Stones, so it's fine. And I'll work on the wife's information from here."

"Let me know when you're here." Lowell was about to hang up. "Oh, I made some headway into The Happy Snappy Marshmallow Company case. We're going to have to move on that soon if we want any chance of recovering the missing funds."

"It's the bookkeeper, isn't it?"

"You're right on the money, Mort. Listen, stay on the line while I punch in the good doctor's birth information and see if it jibes with what you feel."

"Will do, Boss."

Lowell entered Williamson's information into his Solar Fire program. "He's a strange duck. The birth time gives him a four-degree Gemini rising. This is quite a chart, especially for someone in the medical profession. He has five planets and Chiron in Pisces, ruler of medicine, as well as music and fine art. I wouldn't be surprised if Dr. Williamson plays an instrument or paints, and probably quite well."

Lowell paused to review the chart in his hand. He smoothed the thinning hair on the top of his head, and patted the ponytail. He didn't like to think he was a vain man, but he knew otherwise.

He continued. "Neptune, ruler of medicine, is in his 6th house of employment in opposition to a 12th house Jupiter. Great potential in any Neptune-ruled areas. Definitely the chart of someone who belongs in the health field. However, those Pisces planets are in opposition to Uranus, Pluto, and Mars in a grouping in Virgo. The opposition of Pluto shows that Dr. Williamson has a strong personality, with a need for power. He is controlling, unbending, and capable of great deception. He's tremendously willful and plays by his own rules. The opposition of Uranus and Mars to the Sun indicates an explosive nature, possibly violent. He doesn't handle authority well, unless *he* is the authoritative figure."

Mort had taken it all in, the new information jibing with his own instinct upon meeting the man in the office. "I picked up a bad temper when I first saw him. And that briefcase! He's a piece of work."

"Undoubtedly. He has the capacity for outbursts and even violence. This is a difficult person to deal with on a day-to-day basis. And his idea of what's ethical may be questionable." *Hence a million dollars cash to do his bidding,* thought Lowell.

"Does this help you locate his wife and child?"

"Indirectly," said Lowell. "I still need the mother's chart to do the job. But Williamson's chart will show me things about his wife through his 7th house, and the children through his 5th house. When I get the wife's chart, I'll look at all the different connections and then add it up."

"So what do you think?"

"All this confirms what I felt from the man when I met him. There's something very powerful and hidden in his personality, as the opposition of Pluto to the Sun shows quite clearly."

"I had the same reaction when I met him. He's not quite what he appears to be. And it would take a personality such as this to leave one million dollars cash with a total stranger and not even want a receipt."

Silence on the phone.

"Mort, we need to find the wife ASAP."

Chapter Five

Sarah buzzed. "Mort again. He's on a roll."

"I found Williamson's wife's birth date."

"Well done, Mort. Not that I ever doubted you. Any difficulty?"

"Not as much as I had with the good doctor, but still most information about both of their lives since their marriage seems to have been wiped out."

"Strange."

"Definitely."

"How did you find it?"

"I found her maiden name and used that. It was simple to access what I needed from the time before she met Williamson."

"Seems easy enough. So why didn't Williamson send me this information?"

"Maybe he's testing you."

"With so much at stake? I doubt it." Lowell turned to his computer. "Tell me what you have."

"She was born on September 11th, 1969 at 7:29 a.m. in New York City."

"Good. Now I can really get to work."

Lowell entered the information into Solar Fire. He looked over the chart and made a few notes.

"What do you see?" asked Mort.

Lowell projected the chart onto the flat-screen TV and began. "Gloria's natal chart reveals a complex person. She's a Virgo with the Sun in the 12th house of the unconscious, where much is hidden. This house is ruled by Pisces and is considered the house of self-undoing, frustration and confinement. It's also called the house of karma, where the lesson is one of service or suffering. People with this placement frequently prefer to work in the background and out of the intrusive eye of the public. She's also a dark of the moon child born right before the New Moon. Much of her life is spent trying to complete things and tie up loose ends. With the Sun, Moon, the south node, and Pluto all in the 12th house, it's difficult for her to express herself at times, and she probably has a bad self-image. The Sun rules the father in the chart. This placement indicates a powerful, but distant, father who could intimidate her. Yet she is drawn to powerful men who remind her of him.

"Mercury conjuncts Jupiter in the 1st house. This is usually an optimistic aspect. She's intelligent and can be quite charming and outgoing when she feels sure of herself. Unfortunately she doesn't often feel that self-confident. Self-doubt and insecurity, strong aspects of her personality, dampen that optimism. She's much more intelligent than people expect and her mind moves much quicker than she often lets on."

Mort smiled to himself as he recognized a kindred spirit.

"Mars squares those Virgo planets, which could make her even less sure of herself and at times quite fearful. She has a temper, but probably hides it, holds it back, because of that Sun and Moon 12th house placement. Mars rules her 3rd house of speech, and it's difficult for her to express herself, even with Mercury conjunct Jupiter, which is usually very positive for communication. Neptune rules her 7th house of relationships, which shows that she will often play the victim in her one-on-one relationships and she's drawn to men who can be deceitful and remind her of her father. It's very difficult for Gloria to stand up for herself, especially to the men in her life.

"With Chiron in the 7th house of relationships, marriage would be difficult, and she would be inclined not to divorce.

San Diego Public Library
DATE DUE SLIP
****

Date due: 9/30/2014,23:59
Title: The sound and the furry
Call number: [MYST] FIC/QUINN
Item ID: 31336092672675
Date charged: 9/9/2014,15:27

Date due: 9/30/2014,23:59
Title: The drowning spool
Call number: [MYST] FIC/FERRIS
Item ID: 31336095310398
Date charged: 9/9/2014,15:27

Date due: 9/30/2014,23:59
Title: Evil in the 1st house : a
Starlight Detective Age
Call number: [MYST] FIC/LEWIS
Item ID: 31336096426391
Date charged: 9/9/2014,15:27

Total checkouts for session:3
Total checkouts:6

<><><><><><><><><><><>
Renew at
www.sandiegolibrary.org
OR Call 619-236-5800 or
858-484-4440 and press 1
then 2 to RENEW. Your
library card is needed to
renew borrowed items.

She would rather stay in an uncomfortable relationship and suffer, than leave.

"The Virgo Moon may very well be her saving grace. While the aspects to the Moon are difficult, Virgo energy tends to think rather than feel. Since the Moon rules the emotions, normally we would like to see it in a more sympathetic sign. But not in this case. Its placement in Virgo allows her to intellectualize her emotions and to create some distance between what is happening and how she feels about it. This is something the chart indicates she would need in order to balance out the rest of her personality. She will respond to emotional situations through her thoughts, not just forming a gut reaction. And that, in some ways, helps her to cope."

When he was done he put the chart in his folder and turned off the TV.

"Mort, we're going to have to find her quickly. Call when you're back."

"Will do." He hung up.

Lowell then printed out about a dozen other charts: synastry and composites between the mother, her husband, and her twins.

The evening ahead promised tedious work that Lowell hated. He had spent much of the past three decades staring at astrology charts of one sort or another. Becoming a private detective was supposed to alleviate the boredom. Sometimes it did. Sometimes it didn't. Like now.

Sarah came in a little before six carrying a shoe box. "I'm leaving in a few minutes. I got a date." She smiled broadly. "I met him in my acting class."

"Is he nice?"

"I think so. I don't know him very well yet. But I'll get his birth information before the night's out."

Lowell laughed. "I'm sure you will. Where are you going?"

"A movie premier. He's got a friend in SAG who gets free tickets." She opened the shoe box and held out a pair of silver glittered shoes with three-inch heels. "What do you think? They're Charlotte Olympia. Cost a fortune." She sat in the chair and put them on. Then she stood up and walked around like a shoe model.

"They're very nice. But don't you have enough shoes? From what you tell me you've got about ninety pairs."

Sarah shook her head. "There's no such thing as enough shoes." She giggled.

"Have a nice time. And tomorrow, if you're still interested in this guy, we'll peek up his skirt a little."

"Will you be alright here alone? Maybe you should go home to the townhouse. This could be a very crazy week and you'll need to be rested."

He took her hands in his. "Thank you for caring. But I'll be fine. I've got work to catch up on, and I can do it better here."

"Okay, Boss. I'll see you in the morning."

Lowell ordered dinner from Louie's and settled in for a night in the office. When he was enmeshed in a case he would some-times stay put for days to avoid distractions. The leather couch was a pull-out with a king-sized orthopedic mattress. His private bathroom contained a full-sized tub and shower, and a small but complete modern kitchen was hidden behind one of the doors. He opened the couch, popped a bottle of Beck's, and worked until almost three. Two more Beck's and the last of the eggplant parm from Louie's. Then he took a hot bath and went to sleep.

Chapter Six

When Sarah buzzed him in the morning he was already showered and on his second cup of coffee. The morning was devoted to studying Dr. and Mrs. Williamson's natal and composite charts. By noon Lowell found what he was looking for. He took the wife's birth chart then "relocating" the chart to various cities on the East Coast. This is done by using the local sidereal time, or moving the time of the chart until the moon is at the exact same place it is in the natural birth chart. By studying each he finally concluded that Gloria Williamson was most likely living within a few miles of Hartford, Connecticut, probably to the west. This was the town that offered her the best chance of employment. He buzzed Mort, who appeared moments later.

"Mort, it's time for you to surf the big Internet waves. Williamson was right about his wife and child. They do appear to be living on the East Coast in the area around Hartford. Find them."

"Not much to go on."

"Well, we know that she's a registered nurse. But she is certainly living under an alias, and it may be hard for her to find work in most hospitals. Look into private ones and agencies that handle nurses, especially those that operate a bit under the radar."

Mort nodded. "I'll go back to when they separated and work forward. I'll let you know when I find something." He left.

Lowell hit the buzzer. "Sarah, get Melinda for me. Try her office and cell phone."

Soon the phone rang.

"Hi, Dad, you called?"

"Are you free anytime today? I need to see you."

"I have to be up in your 'hood about two o'clock. Will you be around?"

"My 'hood?"

"Sorry, been doing a lot of pro-bono work."

"I'll be here."

Melinda was dressed in a short blue skirt, a ruffled white shirt cut rather low, and large pearls. When Lowell saw her he did a double take.

"A little dressy for the afternoon, don't you think?"

She laughed. "I have to go to a semi-formal cocktail party at five. No time to change. Besides, it can't hurt my relationship with my clients."

"Yes," said her father, "your male clients."

She laughed again. "Oh, Dad. So what's going on? Why did you need to see me so quickly?"

"I want to hire you to do some legal work. If you have the time."

"This is a first. You're lucky. At the moment I'm only moderately busy as the junior associate. About fourteen hours a day. What's up?"

He turned the computer screen off, stood up, and stretched. "Let's take a walk. It's a beautiful summer day and I could use a little fresh air. Are those fancy shoes good for walking?"

"Yes, Dad." She looked down and pointed at her feet. "They may be fancy, but I only wear flat, comfy shoes. I hate heels. I'm definitely tall enough." She winked. "Let's go."

They walked to First Avenue so as not to be jostled by the midtown madness. Nannies and strollers surrounded them, and a view of the East River between buildings gave a false sense of bucolic serenity. It was in the mid-eighties, warm, but compared to the oppressive record-setting heat of the past July, it felt almost spring-like.

As they passed a Starbucks, Lowell stopped. "Want some coffee?"

"Sure."

They got their caffeine fix, hers iced, and headed north again.

Melinda took a big draw through her straw. "So what's this all about?"

"You know that case I've been working on?"

"The doctor with the million dollars?"

He nodded. "I need you to find out what legal rights his estranged or possibly divorced wife has in the matter."

"Okay. Tell me about it."

Lowell took a sip. Still too hot. He tossed the top in a garbage can, and blew on the coffee several times. "Dr. and Mrs. Williamson have been living apart for many years, ever since the boys were very small. As I told you, according to Williamson she grabbed one of the babies and took off. I still don't know why. Now that Williamson has hired me to find them for a kidney transplant scenario, I want to know exactly what I'm getting myself into."

"I see your predicament. You don't want to find the wife and child without gaining some legal protection, in case things aren't quite what they seem and you wind up in the middle of a custody battle."

"Smart little cookie."

"And your legal counsel."

"Right."

"I'll need a retainer to make this on the up-and-up. How is five dollars?"

With his free hand, Lowell reached into his pocket, flipped open a small bundle of bills, and Melinda pulled a five from the batch.

"Okay, now I'm your lawyer. What can I do for you?"

"Brush up on abandonment in a marriage and issues about custody when a marriage dissolves or the parents live apart."

"Pretty broad topic. Anything in particular?"

"I just want to be ready for whatever develops. For example, can one parent take a child out of state or insist on a medical procedure without the written consent of the other?"

"Okay." She looked at her watch. "Yikes, got to scoot."

Melinda hailed a cab. "I can come up to the townhouse after the cocktail party, if you like, say around seven."

Lowell smiled. "Great. We can have dinner and chat."

She hopped into the cab and disappeared.

Lowell spent the rest of the day working in the office. His over-sized mahogany and leather desk could barely hold the piles of charts as he sifted from one to another. When he needed to study one up close he would bring it up on the TV screen. Thelonious Monk's unique piano style was playing softly in the background; his bizarre syncopation complementing Lowell's rather strange thought patterns.

At six he called Andy and went to the townhouse. Normally he would be staying in the office again, but a private dinner with his daughter wasn't something he would readily give up.

He opened the front door. "Hello, anyone here?"

Julia came out of the kitchen. "Hello, Mr. Lowell, Melinda is upstairs. Would you like a drink? I'm preparing dinner."

"Thank you, Julia. I'll have a beer. What room is she in?"

"She went up to the third floor to freshen up. She should be down shortly."

He went into the living room and sat in a plush, velvet blue armchair. He picked up that day's *New York Times*, turned to the crossword puzzle, took a pen and began filling it in. He had done the *Times* puzzle in pen since he was a teenager. Julia returned with a Spatan beer and a chilled pilsner glass. She set them down on coasters on the table next to the couch. Lowell preferred to pour his own beer. He liked a head on it and many people thought that the top of a beer should be flat. He poured it to his liking and was taking the first sip when Melinda appeared.

He nodded. "Want a drink?"

She smiled. "Sure. It's been a rough day. I'll have a martini."

Lowell started to rise.

"Don't, Dad. I'll get my own. And Julia has enough to do."

She returned shortly with a chilled martini glass and a small pitcher. She set the glass on a coaster and poured in the elixir carefully.

"Ah, delightful." She sipped and put the glass down in the center of the coaster. "So tell me about this."

Lowell took a healthy swig of his beer. "I believe I can find the elusive Mrs. Williamson and her son. I just want to make sure that things go as planned. And I want the best attorney I can get. That's why I put you on retainer."

"Speaking of which, I found a check in my purse."

Lowell smiled. "You didn't know I was a magician as well as a detective? Yes, I snuck it in there while you were upstairs."

"But it's for five thousand dollars, and we agreed on five, cinco, cinq dollars."

He shrugged. "A few extra zeros."

"I've told you I don't need your money."

"This isn't charity. I'm hiring you and I expect you to do a professional job. It's my neck on the chopping block. Your time is valuable and if I'm going to make use of it I'll make it worth your while."

"Whatever."

"Hey, I'm getting paid a million dollars. The least I can do is spread the wealth. If you want, give half to charity, same as me."

"I will."

She got up and walked to a breakfront, opened it and took out a tall, pine-scented candle. "It reminds me of Christmas. You don't mind?"

He shook his head. But the truth was that sometimes sensory input could thrust him into the past, and depending on his state of mind, that could be a dangerous place.

As she brought the candle to the table, the subtle smell hit him, and he found it pleasant and unthreatening. He relaxed.

She lit the candle. "So, where is she?"

"I believe she's in Connecticut, near Hartford. As soon as Mort finds her, I'll go up and talk to her. This isn't the type of case I would usually take, so I'm feeling my way."

She pointed her martini glass at him. "You know why you took this case, don't you?"

"Am I going to get a lot of psycho-babble now?"

"I did minor in psychology after all."

"Well, practice it on someone else. I took the case because it interested me."

"Uh huh. You know, Dad, for someone so smart and aware…"

Julia came in from the kitchen. Through the open door the fragrant aroma of dinner escaped. "Mr. Lowell, dinner's ready. Where do you want to eat?"

"How about the little nook outside the kitchen?" It was a table just for two. "And Julia, I've told you to call me David."

"Yes, Mr. Lowell. I'll set the table. It'll be about five minutes." She went back into the kitchen. They could hear the welcoming sounds of plates and silverware as Julia arranged the table.

"What would you do without her?"

Lowell finished his beer. "I don't want to find out."

The house phone rang.

Mort.

"I found her."

Chapter Seven

It was a dreary, drizzly day. Dark clouds hung over the city like the soft filter on a camera lens. The long drive to Hartford lay ahead, so Lowell wanted to stretch his legs a bit. As he walked uptown the glare of lights from the oncoming cars cast ominous shadows on the damp streets and buildings. New York's avenues are caverns laid between mountainous structures, unending and relentless. To truly walk the streets of Manhattan one had to have a hiker-explorer mentality. And Lowell often felt like a traveler within his own city—trekking along its well-trodden paths, into distant villages with new and exciting discoveries.

He called Andy for a pickup in front of Eli's Bakery as he turned down East Ninety-first Street and entered the store. Lowell loved the smell of fresh baking bread as it emanated from the bakery department sending shivers of childhood nostalgia through him. His mother often baked on rainy afternoons.

He walked into the café by the front door and ordered a banana croissant to go. He didn't like their coffee, found it bitter. He'd get Starbucks later. Then he meandered through the store waiting for Andy's text. There were exotic goodies from all over the world that piqued his interest. The owner of the store, Eli, had had a falling out with his family, the owners of Zabar's, many years before and opened this place. The prices always shocked Lowell, and he wondered how they could charge eight bucks for the exact same licorice you can get in the supermarket for

$2.99. Lowell also found the prices at Zabar's to be outlandishly inflated. Probably a lot of over-expansive Jupiter energy in that family tree.

His phone beeped. He walked outside and the limo pulled up alongside him.

The driver's window whirred down.

"Where to boss?"

"Andy, good morning. We're going to West Hartford. Here's the address."

From the car, Lowell made his morning trades to help pass the time.

"Roger, I'm getting back into cotton. Venus is about to enter Libra, and that's usually a bullish signal."

"Okay, how many?"

Lowell looked at his notes and account information. "Buy me twenty, market-on-open, and put a stop in at 63.20. Then put a buy for twenty more at 65.00 with the same stop out, good-till-cancelled."

"I've been looking at cotton too. I think I'll follow your lead. I'll call you with your fills."

"Okay, thanks."

Lowell sat back and in his mind replayed the conversation with Mort from last night.

"You were right," said Mort. "She's working as a private nurse under a different name."

"So where is she?"

"West Hartford, like you thought. She's working at a residence taking care of an elderly man. And she's living in an apartment complex just outside the city limits. Here's the address."

"How did you find her?"

"Once you gave me the general vicinity I hacked into the local hospitals in the area, there's only a few, and looked for patients that needed home care. Based on her age and what little we know about her I was able to narrow it down. A few discreet phone calls, and some luck, and bingo. The name she's using turns out to be deceased. I figured, that's our gal."

The rain was making Lowell depressed, so he turned a few knobs. The windows darkened for a moment and then lit up with a sunny, beautiful scene from the California coast. The windows were fitted with plasma screens that were transparent when turned off, but when they were activated they projected a very real filmed scene and even took on the same physical characteristics. Now they were warm to the touch, reflecting the California climate. Lowell could swear he felt the sun's rays streaming through the window. This was an invention his client and friend Walter Delaney had created. Until the bugs were worked out and the patents secured, Lowell was one of the few people operating the mechanism. It had proven quite a useful trick on several cases.

He rode in silence staring out the window at the faux-ocean view, wondering what it would be like to live somewhere else. New York City was the only home he knew, but sometimes change was freeing. Maybe it was time to consider an adjustment.

About ninety minutes later Andy buzzed him. "We're almost there."

Lowell turned off the window screens and looked back out at the overcast suburban landscape.

They got off the highway and Andy followed the GPS instructions until they were in front of an unexceptional square, brick apartment building probably built in the sixties.

Lowell got out of the car and took a deep breath. The suburbs smelled clean and fresh. He didn't usually notice how thick and invasive the city air was until he got away from it.

He took the elevator to the thirteenth floor, got out, read the room numbers, and turned left. At room number 1345 he knocked. There was no response. He knocked again.

The door opened. "Yes, may I help you?" A short, very thin, middle-aged woman with graying brown hair peeked from behind the door.

"Are you Gloria Williamson?"

She stared at him. "No. There's nobody here by that name." She began to close the door.

"If I could find you, don't you think others can?"

She stopped. "He sent you, didn't he?"

Lowell nodded briefly.

The woman put her hand to her brow. "I was afraid of this."

Lowell shook his head. "I assure you, I have no intention of revealing your whereabouts unless you wish it."

She looked at him for a moment then waved him in. It was a modest apartment, sparsely furnished with mismatched odds and ends. The couch was a lime green. A well-worn gray armchair stood across the room. The few tables bore lamps of different shapes and sizes.

"Are you a private detective?"

He handed her a card.

"Starlight Detective Agency? David Lowell? I know that name from somewhere." She looked more closely at him. "Oh yes, I saw you on TV recently. You're that astrologer who solved the murder of those rock stars, aren't you? Well Mr. Lowell, now that you've found me, what do you plan to do about it?"

"I don't know. That's up to you."

She sighed. "Please sit down."

He sat in the armchair.

She sat on the couch, retrieving a cup of tea from a low table. "Would you like something? Tea or water?"

"No thank you."

She was a nervous woman, her voice wavering as she spoke. "So he sent you to find me. After all these years I was hoping he'd given up."

Lowell remained silent.

"Do you know him well?"

"I only met him once, when he hired me to find you."

She nodded, and then gazed out the window trying to decide what to say next. She turned back toward Lowell. "He's a monster. You can't possibly know what he's like."

Lowell nodded. "Why don't you tell me about it?"

She got up and began to pace. "I don't know. Why should I trust you?"

"There's no reason you should. Just tell me what you feel comfortable with."

She sat back down and looked at him carefully. "I may regret this, but my instincts tell me I should." She wrung her hands and sighed. "I don't know where to start."

"How about at the beginning?"

"Well, I suppose so." She kept wringing her hands as she spoke, trying in vain to wash away some unseen blemish. "At first I guess we had a normal marriage. There were a few disagreements, and I suppose the usual struggles as we got to know each other. He was fairly easygoing and generous when we were dating. But then soon after we were married he started to change."

"How so?"

"It was subtle at first. Some mood swings, an occasional argument that seemed irrational to me. But I was young and didn't understand much about relationships. As the months went by, he became more abusive. He has a terrible temper, which at first he hid from me. It started to come out more and more. He would scream at me, sometimes in public. But then it escalated. He…" she stopped to catch her breath. "He would hit me, sometimes very hard."

"What did you do?"

"I tried to talk to him, begged him to seek help. But he just said it was a bad mood and he'd get over it."

"Did he continue to hit you?"

She nodded. "Many times. Even when I was pregnant. Once he threatened to push me down the stairs. I became afraid for myself and my unborn children. I needed to know who this man was that I had married. Everyone thought he was a god. People came from all over for his advice and skills as a surgeon. But I had to live with another side of his personality. I didn't know what to do. I had very few friends and no money of my own. I felt trapped. I needed to learn more about the father of my children.

"One night Edgar and I went to a charity ball where I met my husband's accountant and his wife, Nancy. She and I hit it off right away and soon became close friends. Several weeks later over lunch I took a chance and confined in her about my troubles. Nancy was very sympathetic. She'd been married before to an abusive man and understood what I was going through. That night when her husband was asleep she opened Edgar's file on her husband's computer and emailed it to me. I was shocked. He was immensely wealthy, something he'd kept from me. I knew we weren't poor, but I had no idea how much money he had. He'd spent years researching genetic diseases and by the time we got married was losing interest in practicing medicine. He was only interested in collecting and patenting rare genes. I later found out that he had been accused of using his wealth to buy, steal, and bully the rights to genetic material from those unfortunate enough to be in possession of a blood type or genetic code that he needed for his work."

Gloria blew out a deep breath that held years of pressure and sadness.

"As the months went by and my due date came closer, he became less violent, as if the children were the important thing. But I knew his anger was bubbling under the surface. I began to realize that I couldn't let him near my children. I didn't know if he was using drugs or what the problem was."

They were quiet for a few moments as Lowell digested the information. Finally he said: "I understand. Tell me more."

She sat silently for a few moments staring past Lowell, her eyes unfocused, looking at a view from her past only she could see.

"After my sons were born he became worse than ever. It was as if my giving birth to his offspring was all he'd been interested in and he had no more use for me. There were some complications from the births and I was forced to remain in the hospital for several weeks. At least the children stayed with me, at first. Edgar came into my room one night, his face flush with anger, his breath smelling from alcohol. He told me that it was time to wean the boys from me. That's the term he used, like they were a litter of animals. That's when I knew I had to get away from him."

She stood up and began pacing again, her agitation quite pronounced.

"Being the doctor's wife does come with some privileges in the hospital. I arranged for an early morning discharge the following day, convincing the nurses that my husband had just forgotten to tell them. Nancy agreed to come by and pick me up with a suitcase of clothing for me and the kids. We were going to start a new life."

Gloria Williamson stopped, closed her eyes, took a deep breath, and looked directly at Lowell. "It was the worst day of my life. The day I lost my son. I still have nightmares."

"Take your time. I know this is painful. But I need to know what happened."

"It was very early. The sun wasn't up yet. It was quiet outside the hospital. Nancy pushed me out in a wheelchair. I was still very weak, and the hospital's regulations demanded it. She had parked just down the street and was holding both babies, as I eased myself into the car.

"Just then, another car squealed to the curb and a very large man I'd seen around the hospital ran to us and grabbed one of the babies. He tried to get the other but my friend twisted away and started to scream bloody murder. I tried to scream too, but the shock of what was happening was too much for me and I couldn't utter a sound. I saw one of my babies…" She closed her eyes again, and kept them closed. "He took off with my child…"

"You don't have to say more. I understand your loss." Lowell had a catch in his throat. "I understand your loss," he repeated, more softly.

She sat back on the couch, spent. "I've been running ever since, forced to adopt aliases and always on my guard. He has unlimited resources, I have few. I couldn't let him come and take my other son. And I knew he wouldn't be happy with just one."

They both sat quietly for a moment. Lowell broke the silence. "How did you survive?"

"For years I roamed around the country taking any job I could find. We lived in California for a while, in terrible places.

I was afraid to work as a nurse, figuring he'd find me that way. But after so many years, the only job I could find that paid decently was back here, so I finally took a chance. I had to use my deceased friend's identity. And now he's found me anyway."

She sat back on the couch and was silent for a while, gazing into space. "How is my other son?"

Lowell shook his head. "That's why I'm here. He's very ill and needs a kidney transplant. He has a very rare blood type from your husband's side."

She nodded. "Oh my God, no!"

Lowell gave her time to process this awful news.

She began to speak again, very slowly, her voice cracking. "I found out about Kevin's blood type when he was about three. I had to take him to a clinic for a horrible cough and they discovered it. They wanted me to keep a supply of his blood just in case something happened."

"Did you?"

"No. I couldn't afford it. I haven't had health insurance since I left him. Mr. Lowell, do you know how expensive it is? It would cost me more than my rent to cover Kevin and me. Some states have programs for poor people, but if I signed up for it he would have been able to find me."

"Your husband hired me to find his son's twin in the hope of convincing you to allow the operation."

"My poor boy, my poor, poor boy." She got up, walked over to the kitchen area, and put her tea cup in the sink. Then she poured herself a glass of water. "You sure I can't get you anything?"

"No, thank you."

She remained standing. "I don't know what to do. I can't let my son die, but I just don't trust that man. Are you sure this isn't just a ruse for him to get Kevin away from me?"

"For the past year Edward has been in and out of a private hospital your husband owns in New Jersey. According to your husband he seems to be fading fast. Also, my astrological interpretation of his chart shows that he is quite susceptible to kidney disease."

Tears welled up in her eyes.

"Mrs. Williamson, Why don't you take a little time and think about it?"

She sipped the water. "Are you going to tell him that you found me?"

"Not unless you want me to."

"But he hired you."

Lowell smiled humorlessly. "That matters less than you think."

"My other son needs me. I can't just turn my back on him."

"Where is your son, if I may ask?"

"He's out with some friends. Kevin's a very sociable young man."

"So what do you want me to do?"

"I suppose I'll have to see Edgar. Would you arrange it? And can we do it somewhere safe? I'm very afraid of him."

"I'll arrange a meeting at my office in Manhattan. Would that be okay?"

She nodded.

He stood up and shook her hand. "You have my number on my card. Why don't you call me when you're ready to meet?"

"You're very kind. I'll call you in a day or so."

Andy drove him back to the city. Lowell didn't turn on his visual playground, but sat looking out at the gray world.

Chapter Eight

When they got back to Manhattan, Lowell decided to take a walk. The clouds had lifted, but it wasn't sunny, just a brighter shade of hot gray. Weather conducive to deep thought.

"Andy, drop me on Fourteenth Street. I'm going to stroll through the Village."

Andy took the FDR to the Twenty-third Street exit and went down Second Avenue. At Fourteenth Street he pulled over and Lowell got out. It was good to stretch his legs. Perhaps he'd become too complacent lately, relying on Andy too much. He was going to see Katherine soon. That thought made him nervous, like a sixteen-year-old kid anticipating a first date.

He walked down Second Avenue, turned right onto Tenth Street, and headed west. He noticed subtle changes each time he come downtown, regretting the modernization that had slowly crept into this mostly unaltered district. But he knew this area was soon going to be massively redefined. NYU was about to gobble up huge chunks in a land grab unprecedented in this city since the heyday of Robert Moses who, two generations before had ripped entire communities from their homes and tore down neighborhood after neighborhood in the name of progress. Some of it was a necessary pruning for legitimate expansion and growth. But some was just wanton ego-fueled destruction.

Something was bothering Lowell. Like eyes, unseen, glaring at the back of his head. He turned around quickly, but nobody seemed to be watching him. A woman was looking in a dress shop window. A homeless man sat outside a deli with a large plastic container hoping for donations. Otherwise the street was very quiet on this hot and muggy day. It wasn't like him to be jittery. But despite a lack of supporting evidence he remained unnerved.

He walked past the Albert on University and Tenth Street. Originally built in the late nineteenth century as the Albert Hotel, it was now a residential apartment building, but was once a meeting center for important writers and artists of their day. Some of its famous guests included Robert Louis Stevenson, Mark Twain, Walt Whitman, Anais Nin, Jackson Pollack, and many others.

He crossed Fifth Avenue and went down to Bleecker Street. Of course this was no longer the center of bohemian music, literature, and politics it had once been. The days of starving artists living in cheap walk-ups while writing novels or perfecting their jazz were gone. The rise in housing prices had long ago pushed them out. Now it was another upper-middle-class paragon, with its romantic winding streets and hidden alleys, and rents in the thousands.

If not for the tireless efforts of Jane Jacobs, a woman with a mission, determined to stop Moses' relentless destruction and renovation, the West Village, with its hundred-year-old buildings and its old European-style charm would have been decimated by the wrecker's ball and replaced by the massive Lower Manhattan Expressway Moses had planned. The Isaacs-Hendrix House built in 1799 still stood at 77 Bedford Street. The Greek revival rowhouses that still lined the north side of Washington Square were built around 1832. They all would have been demolished if Robert Moses had had his way.

In the Fifties this area was home to Jack Kerouac, James Baldwin, Truman Capote, and so many other writers of that era. Dylan Thomas, who collapsed at the Chelsea Hotel after a night of drinking at the White Horse Tavern, died at St. Vincent's Hospital on West Twelfth Street. St. Vincent's was closed now, leaving the area without a single full-service hospital. Its buildings were being redesigned as another upper-class residence.

And in the 1960s, the final surge of creativity to emerge from this incredible neighborhood attracted the likes of Jimi Hendrix, Theloneous Monk, Simon and Garfunkel, Phil Ochs, Dave Von Ronk, Joni Mitchell, Bob Dylan, and Peter, Paul, and Mary…the list was endless. *It's very unlikely that another great musical explosion will ever emerge from the West Village again,* he thought. *No struggling artist could afford to live there. And the clubs that nurtured them have mostly been priced out of existence.* There was so much history here, something ignored by realtors and corporations who could only see the bottom line and not the human value.

Walking was always one of Lowell's greatest pleasures. No gadgets, no gimmicks, no car. Just him and his feet, freedom personified. He crossed Seventh Avenue and went down Bank Street, one of the loveliest of all, seemingly untouched by time. Remove the cars and you could easily think you'd awakened in 1880.

What a strange pair of cases, he thought. *A missing woman who, it turns out had good reason to go missing. A sick child, a twin no less. A million dollars in cash and a family reunited whatever the end result.*

And the embezzlement of the retirement money so many people relied on for their old age. That's cold, he said quietly to himself, *very cold. And a marshmallow company, to boot!*

After several hours of meandering, he'd had enough. His mind was clear and he was ready for work once again. A quick text and soon he was heading uptown with Andy.

Chapter Nine

"Mrs. Williamson is on line one."

He picked up the phone. "Yes, Mrs. Williamson?"

It was 9:01 a.m. *How thoughtful yet eager,* Lowell thought. *Both good signs.*

"I'm ready to meet with Edgar and see what this is all about. I can't just let one of my boys die. The sooner the better."

"Certainly. I'll try to get in touch with him now. When are you free to come?"

"I've cleared my schedule for the next few days, so anytime you can arrange it from today through next week would be fine. I could even be there in an hour if you wanted. I'm in Westchester visiting a friend. She has a son about Kevin's age so we're staying here for a few days. I had to get out of the apartment. And they've got a pool, which is just great for Kevin."

"Okay, I'll let you know." They hung up.

Lowell buzzed Sarah. "Get me Dr. Williamson. If he doesn't answer, leave a message that I've found his wife and son."

A few moments later Sarah buzzed. "Dr. Williamson on line one."

Lowell picked up the phone. "Dr. Williamson, I've located your wife. She would like me to arrange a meeting with you in my office."

"That's very good news, Mr. Lowell. When can we set this up?"

"She would like it to be as soon as possible."

"As would I."

"Are you free today?"

"Yes, of course," said Williamson, "I can be at your office at noon, if that works."

"I'll arrange it and have my assistant Sarah confirm it with you."

Lowell sent Andy to pick up Gloria. She arrived at about 11:45 and sat in a client's chair in Lowell's office staring out the window.

"Can I get you something? Coffee, or perhaps something stronger?"

She turned toward him, a faraway look in her eyes and shrugged. "I guess coffee would be nice, thank you."

He buzzed Sarah. "Would you please get Mrs. Williamson a cup of coffee with…"

"Milk and two sugars."

"…milk and two sugars. And I'll have one as well."

Sarah came in a few minutes later with the coffee in delicate china cups she used mostly for clients, and a plate of cookies. "I thought you might like something with your coffee." She put the snacks on the table by the couch and left.

Lowell got up from his desk. "Let's sit over here on the couch."

Gloria displayed little animation and seemed almost in a trance. She sipped her coffee, took one of the cookies and nibbled the tiniest bite. Her demure attitude belied a rather attractive woman in her forties. Her face was quite pretty and if she'd paid any attention at all to her looks she could be very desirable. But she carried herself in a shy, reserved manner and dressed in frumpy clothes that hid any sexuality she might accidentally exude.

Lowell could see her distress. "I'm sure you're worried about your sons. It'll be okay."

Gloria looked at him. "I don't trust that man. I can't."

"I understand. I'll stay with you the entire time if you wish."

"I would like that very much. I'm only agreeing to see him because of you. I've always been a believer in astrology, and your demeanor and reputation are very comforting."

He nodded in thanks. "I'll be around as long as you need me."

The intercom rang. Lowell walked over to the receiver. "Yes, Sarah?…Okay." He turned to Gloria. "It's your husband." He switched phone lines. "Yes, Dr. Williamson. I have your wife here with me…I see…Do you wish to talk to her?…Okay." He hung up.

"He's running a bit late. He'll be here in half an hour."

She nodded silently. They finished the coffee.

"I have some work to do. There are magazines and a TV in the conference room. Anything you need, please tell Sarah and she'll see to it." Lowell ushered her out to Sarah's desk.

About thirty minutes later the intercom buzzed.

"Dr. Williamson is here."

"Have him come in. And then please get Mrs. Williamson."

The door opened and Williamson entered. "Well, Mr. Lowell, your reputation is well earned. That was quick work. But our deal is still the same. You've earned your money."

Before Lowell could respond, Sarah led Gloria in. When she saw her ex-husband she gasped audibly.

"Gloria," he said, "so nice to see you again. How have you been?"

There was no discernable warmth in his voice. Lowell thought he could have been talking to a stranger he'd encountered for a second time on a train, not the mother of his children.

Williamson went over to hug Gloria, but she backed away.

"As you wish. We have important business to discuss that concerns us both. As you know, Edward is very sick. Without a kidney transplant I'm afraid he won't last more than a few more weeks."

She nodded.

Williamson continued. "Because of a quirk of fate, the boys have inherited my unusual blood type and finding another donor has proven daunting. My left kidney was damaged in a car accident a number of years ago, and Kevin is the only possible solution at this point."

"I understand."

"So you agree to the operation?"

Gloria bit her lower lip. "The final decision must be Kevin's. It's his body, after all. And I assume he has legal rights in the matter as well."

Williamson's impatience was obvious. "A decision has to be made, and soon, or your other son will die. Now let's get this thing done before it's too late." Lowell had a chance to see the doctor's aggressive demeanor toward his wife.

Gloria seemed deflated. Her shoulders sagged, her eyes unfocused. Finally she looked at her estranged husband. "Like I said, the final decision must be Kevin's."

"Have you told him about this?"

She nodded. "He knows."

"Well, it's time to find out."

"He's at my apartment."

"Then let's go ask him."

"Okay," she sighed.

Lowell stood. "I'll have my driver take us up there."

Williamson stood as well. "I have my own car and prefer to drive there separately."

"Very well. My driver will take us and you can follow."

They all went down to the street where Andy was waiting ever patiently. Lowell helped Gloria into the limo.

"Are you sure you're ready, Gloria?"

She looked at Lowell, tears in her eyes.

"I think so."

Chapter Ten

The ride up was uneventful. Gloria was quiet, withdrawn. There was traffic and it took a bit longer to get there. Lowell would have preferred to turn on a more cheery scene, perhaps the Vermont snowstorm he was so fond of, but he wasn't sure how his guest would respond, so they sat in silence gazing out the window at the overcast day.

When they reached West Hartford, Andy pulled over in front of Gloria's building. Williamson found parking out front. Andy waited with the limo.

Gloria opened the door and they entered the apartment.

Williamson was last in. He closed the door. "Gloria, please get the boy."

She disappeared into the back and returned a few moments later with Kevin. At fifteen he was as tall as his father and looked much older than his years. "Kevin," she said, "this is your father."

Williamson stood in front of him. "Kevin, let me look at you. My God, you're grown into a man. How does the time go by so fast? It's really quite amazing how much you look like Edward. Though much more robust, I'm afraid." He extended his hand.

The boy eyed him cautiously for a moment. Lowell sensed disdain in his bearing. Then he finally stuck out his hand. "Yeah, whatever."

Williamson shook the lad's hand. "You understand what I'm asking of you?"

Kevin nodded. "You want to take one of my kidneys and give it to my brother."

"That's right. You know that you can live a full and uninhibited life with just one kidney, but without this transplant your brother Edward will surely die soon. You'll be saving his life."

"I know. I looked it all up on the Internet."

"Wonderful. I'm glad you did. I'll be doing the operation myself to make sure nothing goes wrong." He smiled a crooked grin. "But this is ultimately your choice. Nobody can make the decision for you. Are you willing to do this?"

Kevin looked at his mother. "Mom, I have to. I only have one brother and he needs my help. I can't turn away. You understand, don't you?"

Gloria grabbed her son and held him tightly. "You've always been a wonderful person, Kevin. I would have been more surprised if you had refused."

She turned to Williamson. "Alright, let's do it."

"Good. I'll make the arrangements at my private hospital. I'll contact you in a few days and let you know when to bring him out."

He turned to his son. "Kevin, you're doing a wonderful thing for your brother and I'm proud of you."

The boy nodded and shrugged. "Got no choice." He looked at his mother, a silent communication transpired between them. Then he put in earphones, turned without saying another word, and went into his room.

"Gloria, no matter what went on between us, this is the right thing to do, and you know it. Please try not to worry. I'll see to it that nothing goes wrong. You're saving your son's life. How can that be a bad thing?"

She just looked him, shaking her head. "I hope you're right."

"Of course I am." He looked at his watch. "I'll leave you alone now. I've got to get back to New Jersey and begin to make preparations. I'll be in touch with you early next week and let you know what day the operation will be. Where can I phone you?"

"Please call Mr. Lowell and let him know. He'll tell me."

"Mr. Lowell, our business has been completed. You've found my other son and have earned your fee. I see no reason for you to be involved in this matter any longer."

Gloria stared at her husband defiantly. "I want him to be involved." She turned to Lowell. "That is, if you're willing to."

Lowell nodded. "I'll help in any way I can."

Williamson shrugged. "If that's what you want Gloria. Very well, Mr. Lowell, I'll get in touch soon."

He turned and headed for the door.

After he left, Gloria collapsed on the couch. "I hope I'm doing the right thing."

Lowell tugged on his ponytail. "I'm sure you are."

"Can you be there at the hospital?"

"Of course. I told you, I won't leave you until you say so."

"I have no money to pay you."

Lowell waved a hand. "I've been more than fairly compensated for my time already. It would be my pleasure to help."

She almost smiled. "Thank you, Mr. Lowell, you're a very kind man."

Lowell was surprised that this had all gone so smoothly. That was the first alarm. He knew it was far from over.

Chapter Eleven

It was early evening when Andy dropped Lowell off at the townhouse. Melinda was sitting on the couch when he entered. He put down his shoulder bag and walked over to her, gave her a kiss on the cheek and sat in his favorite chair. "What are you doing here?"

"I thought I'd stay over and we can leave for mom's place from here in the morning. No reason to make Andy come downtown to get me."

"Well, I'm glad to have you. I'm having a beer. Can I get you something?"

"Yes, that sounds like a good idea. I'll have one too."

Lowell got up and headed for the kitchen. Melinda followed and sat at the square metal table in the corner. Julia had a delicious smelling dinner cooking in the oven and Lowell had to resist the temptation to peek. He took two chilled mugs from the freezer, opened two Spatan beers, and poured them into the icy glasses.

He handed one to Melinda who took a sip. "Umm, very refreshing."

"It's a beautiful night, why don't we eat outside?"

"That would be nice." Melinda opened her purse and took out her checkbook. "I want to return your retainer."

"Don't be silly, you don't have to return it. You've earned it."

"Earned it? I didn't do anything."

"You watched my back. Besides, I'm not sure your work is done."

"Why? You found the boy. This case was pretty simple."

Lowell retied his ponytail. "Yes, too simple."

"What do you mean?" She knew that when he fiddled with his hair it was a sign of discomfort. Something was bothering him.

He took a sip of his beer. "Let's just say this was the easiest million dollars I ever made." He thought for a second. "Well, the second easiest. Buying oil futures at thirty-two dollars a barrel when Pluto was about to enter Sagittarius and holding them until they hit one-hundred-thirty was the easiest. This was the quickest."

"Something's bothering you about this case, isn't it?"

He stroked his chin. "The charts helped me discover where Mrs. Williamson was living, possibly more quickly than I could have otherwise, but I believe that any competent detective could have found her and the child without the use of astrology."

"So why did he come to you?"

Lowell shrugged. "And why offer me far more money than was necessary?"

"What do you think?"

Lowell walked over to the kitchen window and stared out at his tiny backyard estate. He saw a robin sitting on a branch of the sycamore that hung over from the yard next door. A second one landed next to it and they flew off together. "I don't know yet. But something doesn't add up. And I think prudence is called for."

"What are you going to do?"

"I promised to help Mrs. Williamson get through the operation. She doesn't trust her husband and, based on their history, has good reasons not to."

"And you think there's a hidden agenda here?"

Another robin landed on the tree and waited for a while, then flew off alone. *Dating is a hard, lonely business,* thought Lowell, *even for birds.*

"I think I'll just keep you on retainer until this is completed."

"Alright," said Melinda, "I'm here if you need me." She put the check back in her purse.

Lowell took a healthy slug of Spatan. "Have you had a chance yet to look into parental rights and issues of abandonment in a marriage?"

"I've got a legal aid working on it. He's put together a fairly substantial folder on federal laws. I also have him looking at New Jersey's state laws. That's where they got married and where Williamson lives, and state laws may take jurisdiction."

They took their beers out to the backyard and sat under the giant umbrella.

The sun was just starting to set to the west. Melinda watched as the shadows moved slowly down the side of the wooden fence. She loved the townhouse and this tiny oasis of nature in the middle of Manhattan.

"What are you going to do?" she asked.

Lowell turned to her and smiled a warm, fatherly grin. She was the one light in his life that never dulled. His love for his children had always been his greatest blessing.

"One challenge at a time. Let's get through this weekend, and then we'll see what next week brings." His instincts told him that the days ahead might hold heartache for many.

Chapter Twelve

At nine sharp on Saturday morning the limo pulled up in front of Lowell's townhouse. David was waiting out front. Andy put the overnight bags in the trunk as Lowell got into the car.

Melinda came down the street, a cardboard tray holding three coffee cups in hand. She gave one to Andy who smiled and held the door as she got into the back. She handed Lowell a Starbucks cup. "I thought you'd like to have this."

"Bless you, girl." He blew on the coffee. "Andy, we're ready when you are."

Andy locked the doors and started driving to the West Side of Manhattan. Even though Lowell lived near the FDR, Andy had found it quicker, easier, and more scenic to drive along the Hudson River. Besides, the FDR led to the dreaded Major Deegan Expressway, which led to the even-more dreaded Cross Bronx Expressway. Calling them expressways was absurd. Driving past Yankee Stadium was cool, but even when there wasn't a home game, traffic was a nightmare. The ten minutes it took to go across town was more than recovered by taking the Henry Hudson Parkway to the Cross County to the New York State Thruway.

"When will the boys have the operation?"

Lowell sipped his coffee. "I expect to hear from Williamson early next week."

Melinda looked closely at her father. "What is it about this case?"

He shrugged. "I'm not sure. As I told you at the beginning, this is a rather unusual case and one that defies definition, so far."

"Give it time to roll around in your brain. You'll figure it out."

The limo was exceptionally equipped for work. Lowell often needed to travel while on a case and staying in touch with his astrology work was essential. There was a full desk with a computer and a swivel chair bolted to the floor. He started to fiddle with the controls at his desk.

"Snowstorm alright with you?"

The windows darkened and then suddenly they were driving through a raging blizzard on the back roads of Vermont. There were twenty-four mini speakers in the limo to create the sound effects associated with the scene being projected. A howling winter wind could be heard in the background.

"You do like your toys, don't you, Dad?"

"This *toy* as you call it has come in handy in several cases."

"Yes, I know."

"And once Delaney works out the kinks and his patents come through, you'll see these in homes, restaurants, and everywhere."

Andy drove them up the New York State Thruway. It was a boring route, and Lowell kept the computer-generated scene in place until they got off the highway and headed down the country roads. Then he turned it off and opened the windows.

It was quiet. Lately Lowell had found the noise of New York City more difficult to bear. The stress level one feels continuously in the big city eventually took its toll. That's why any Manhattanite who could, got out on the weekends. Everyone else headed to a park, or got lost in the Sunday paper.

Melinda leaned out the window and took in a big breath. "This is so much better than your phony movie scene."

"Yes, but this winter when it's snowing and the wind is howling for real you may enjoy a drive along the beach through Southern California."

It took them a little over two and a half hours to get from the city to Woodstock. Andy drove into town down Mill Hill Road onto Route 212, which turned into Tinker Street. The small town feel was refreshing and comforting. Lowell particularly liked the unhurried pace, and when the kids were young, he would take his family there whenever his schedule would allow. He didn't realize how much he'd missed it until now.

Andy took a right onto a small country road and followed it until the dead end. Then he pulled up in front of a pale blue shingled house with a wraparound porch.

Melinda and Lowell got out and stretched their legs. The house bordered the woods and they could hear numerous birds chattering their daily gossip. The front door opened and Catherine came from the house. She was dressed in a pink top, jeans, and sneakers with no laces, her signature casual attire since high school.

Every time Lowell saw her he felt a sense of excitement. When he saw her dressed like that he suddenly felt at home and smiled. She was very beautiful in an earthy way. Her brown hair glistened in the sunlight. Her radiant green eyes were striking. Wherever they went men noticed them and often commented. But then, most men noticed her long before they saw her eyes. At five feet, nine inches she was a little taller than Lowell, but still quite a bit shorter than Melinda. She'd worked as a model in her twenties and kept her fabulous figure through a steady passion of yoga and running.

She went over to her daughter and they hugged. "Let me look at you." She stepped back. "You look tired, and a little thin."

"Oh, Mom, you sound just like Dad, you know that? I'm fine, really."

Catherine laughed. "Yes, we're both your parents. And love you dearly." She turned to Lowell. "David, how are you?"

"Never better. It's good to see you." They hugged, distantly.

"Andy, it's good to see you again, too."

"Hello, Catherine." He picked up the bags. "Where should I put these?"

"Just leave them at the top of the stairs, if you don't mind."

He picked them up. "My pleasure. You've had the house painted since I was here last. It looks great."

"Thank you for noticing." She glanced at her ex-husband.

They went into the house and Andy climbed the stairs with several bags in each hand. Melinda went up with him and settled into her room.

Catherine turned to Lowell. "You look a little tired too."

He smiled. "Maybe just a bit. It gets harder each year to play Sherlock Holmes."

"I'll bet. But you love it, don't you?"

He shrugged.

"How about a cup of coffee?"

"That would be nice. It was a long drive." He followed her into the kitchen. Catherine had inherited the house from her uncle shortly after they got married and they had spent as much time there as schedules allowed. They usually had the holidays there with the kids. Thanksgiving in the woods just seemed so much more appropriate than on East Eighty-third Street. This was their family home. He wondered how many times they had sat in this room through the years. "Andy's right. The place looks great."

"I've been sprucing it up a bit."

They sat at the counter in the center island as Catherine poured two cups of pre-made brew. "How about a slice of pie? I've got a fresh organic cherry I just picked up from the farmer's market."

"You know I've never been able to turn down cherry pie."

She cut two slices and put them on small plates, then sat. "How have you really been, David?"

He ate a bite, and then sipped his coffee. "Okay. It's been a busy summer."

"I know. The rock 'n' roll murder case must have been exhausting." She took a bite of pie. "What are you working on now?"

He told her about Dr. Williamson, the twins, and the million dollars.

"Wow, that's some story." She sipped her coffee and looked at him intently. "This must have been a very difficult case for you, dealing with the potential death of his son. I'm sure it brought up a lot of things."

He nodded. "Yes, I think it's made me revisit Robert's death more than I realized."

"Is that why you took it? It certainly wasn't for the money."

He ate more of the pie. "I suppose so. I haven't really thought it all out yet. But, no, the money wasn't the motivation."

She nodded. "Is that why you wanted to come up?"

He shrugged. "I always try to come up this time of year to visit him."

Melinda came down the stairs and entered the kitchen. She was dressed in blue shorts and a matching shirt. She walked over to the counter, took a cup, and poured herself some coffee from the pot. "Should we go soon? I'd like to be there while there's still daylight."

Catherine finished her coffee and put the cup in the sink. "Let me just get a jacket." She went upstairs and returned shortly wearing a stylish brown cloth jacket with wide lapels and a multitude of seemingly useless pockets and zippers. "I'm ready when you are."

Andy was outside waiting for Lowell's instructions as they walked out of the house.

"Boss, you want me to drive you?"

Lowell shook his head. "No, I think we'll walk. In fact, you're off the clock now. If I need you I'll call. Please make yourself at home."

He nodded. "I'm going to stay with my cousin over in Phoenicia, a few minutes away. Let me know if you need me. I can be here in no time." He got in the limo and took off.

The family walked silently the mile or so to the outskirts of town, lost in their own thoughts.

Chapter Thirteen

There was a slight chill in the air as they stood by the grave. Nobody said a word. There wasn't anything to say. Robert's grave was well kept; Catherine saw to that. She put fresh flowers there every week and paid extra for a caretaker to trim the grass and keep an eye on things. It was on a small rise overlooking the town. Their heads were bent in private solemn contemplation.

Lowell glanced up and noticed a man leaning against a tree watching them. There was something amiss in the man's manner that bothered Lowell. He looked over at his family, somber and introverted, his feelings of protectiveness rising to the surface. His hand automatically went to his cell phone ready to text Andy if anything was wrong. When he looked back, the man was gone. He shrugged. *Must be getting paranoid,* he thought.

As they stood there silently, Lowell reached out his hand to Catherine. At first she shook her head, not bothering to wipe the tears running freely down her face. She turned away from him and looked off toward the sunset. But then without turning back she put her hand out and he took it. They stood like that for a few moments, and then Catherine turned her head toward him. They hugged tightly as if letting go would tear apart the universe. They hugged as one would a sister or a long-lost friend.

Melinda looked up and smiled through her tears. Then she moved off for a walk into town. David and Catherine went back to the house and sat on the front porch for cocktails. The mood was subdued, but not depressed. The tears at the graveside had washed away much of the sadness, leaving a peaceful acceptance in its wake.

Melinda came back shortly and changed into jeans and a flannel shirt tied off at the bottom, her hair pulled back in a ponytail. She was sitting on the front porch swing-couch looking about sixteen. "I ran into Zack today at the bookstore."

"Oh? How's he doing?" Catherine sipped her white wine on the rocks.

"Fine. He looks good. Says he's got a good job with a local computer company. Seems to have put his stuff in order. We're having dinner tonight."

"Oh?"

"Oh, Mom, it's Zack. If anything was going to happen it would have happened long ago. He's like a cousin. I just thought you two could use an evening alone. We'll have all day together tomorrow. Dad, you don't have to be back too early, do you?"

"No. I've got Mort and Sarah holding down the fort. And there's little I can do on Sunday anyway." He sipped his Spatan beer. "I won't hear from Williamson until next week. Even Monday morning would be okay." He looked at Catherine. "If you want the company."

"We'll see. Let's get through dinner first." Catherine looked at Melinda. "Aren't you going to change?"

"Why? This is how I always dress with Zack."

"Maybe that's why nothing ever happened between you."

"Mom!"

◇◇◇

At 7:30 Zack swung by and picked up Melinda. He was also dressed in jeans, with a leather jacket over a plaid shirt.

As they drove away, Catherine turned to David. "They look like an ad for the Grand Ole Opry." She sighed. "I guess Melinda's right. They are more like cousins."

Catherine and David walked to the Farmhouse Restaurant on the edge of town and sat at a table next to the window. There was a magnificent view into a small valley with majestic pines and oaks reaching for the heavens, serene and everlasting, so it seemed.

"I always loved this view." Lowell sipped his Sauvignon blanc. He usually drank what Catherine was drinking when they went out.

"The area's changing."

"So I've heard."

"More construction everywhere you look and the fear of this stupid fracking for gas has most of the locals up in arms."

Lowell shook his head. "Such short-sighted fools. How can you threaten your very environment for a few bucks and a temporary drop in energy prices?"

They both looked out the window, the scene now seeming so much more fragile, perhaps not everlasting after all.

"Do you think she'll ever find someone?"

"Melinda? Her chart certainly gives her plenty of opportunity to find a mate. It's whether she wants one or not."

"You spend much more time with her than I do. What do you think? Is she marriage material? God knows she's pretty enough."

"She was dating someone. I think his name was Peter?"

"David, that was almost two years ago."

"Really? Doesn't seem so long ago."

"It was around the time when that judge got murdered and Melinda brought you that bartender as a client. What ever happened to her?"

"She works at a pet store and seems to be doing quite nicely. I can't believe you know that much about my cases."

"I keep pretty good tabs on you." She sipped her wine. "I understand you spent some time with Vivian Younger." She smirked. "What was that like?"

David took a piece of bread and hurriedly buttered it, then shoved it in his mouth. He needed a moment to think. His brief fling with Vivian Younger wasn't worth confessing to Catherine, even though they were no longer married, but he didn't like lying to her. He chewed, slowly, took a sip of water, and then a sip of wine.

"Spending time with her made me realize just how much I missed you."

She nodded and let it go.

Dinner was good, homey-comfort food. They finished the wine and ordered another bottle. When the table was cleared he sipped his wine and looked into Catherine's beautiful eyes. "You look well."

"So do you."

"Well, I don't know how. I'm too busy to even take care of myself properly." He patted his paunch. "I could really use a short vacation, that's for sure. Remember the last time we went away this time of year?"

She twirled her glass, the ice banging against the sides. "Of course. Fire Island."

He laughed. "We were like two kids. I don't think we'd been away for more than a year at that time. Money was very tight."

"Yes, it was right before you started to make your fortune in the oil deal."

He sipped his drink. "It was wonderful. And…so romantic. I had a great time."

She smiled, but looked at her glass, not at him.

He looked out the window in silence.

She looked at David. "That was a wonderful few days."

Chapter Fourteen

He took her hand across the dinner table. "You've always been so lovely to me. You're the one true love of my life."

She smiled. Then the smile faded and she suddenly pulled her hand back. "Oh no you don't. Attitudes and platitudes," she sipped her wine, "and platypuses. You do this to me every time—you pull me back in. Damn you!" She emptied her glass and reached for the bottle.

Lowell watched silently. She was stepping over the line. He'd seen it a few times before.

The waiter ran over and grabbed the bottle first. "Allow me, ma'am." He started to pour.

Lowell put his hand up. "A double espresso, please."

He looked over at Catherine. She grimaced. Then nodded.

"Make that two double espressos," he said.

After dinner they walked around town, passing the playhouse theatre and houses more than a century old.

She took his arm. "You know, coffee doesn't sober you up. That's a fallacy. It just makes you an awake drunk."

"I'm still in love with you."

"David, you have to stop. It's not going to work. We're just so…we've changed too much."

There was a chill in the air. She pulled the collar up around her neck, and then took his arm again. "You know I still love you. I always will. You're the man in my life, no matter how we describe it. But right now I just can't see us…you know."

They walked in silence through the underbrush, kicking up the few early fallen leaves as they went.

He wanted to pull his collar up as well, but was afraid to let go of her arm. "We must have walked this path a thousand times through the years."

"Um hmm."

"Do you remember that time Melinda fell out of the tree? It was somewhere right around here."

She held on tighter. "Oh sure. That's when she broke her arm. What a to-do that was!"

He laughed. "What was she, about eleven?"

"That's right. She had just had a birthday party that week. She was always such a tomboy."

"I remember Robert came screaming up to the house, he was sure she was..." He stopped.

Catherine looked over at him. "It's okay to say it, David. He was sure she was dead. If we're ever going to get past this we have to face it in all of its subtlety. When someone close leaves you forever the feelings seem to never let go completely." She stopped walking and looked at him. "Losing Robert was such a terrible time. I never thought I'd be able to feel again or enjoy life. But I do."

David was silent.

She leaned her head on his shoulder. "I didn't mean to blame you, really I didn't. I guess I just had to blame someone. And God is just too convenient a scapegoat."

"What could I have done?"

"You've helped people in all areas of their lives. You've predicted dozens of world events, prevented your clients from making the worst mistakes of their lives. Why couldn't you have done the same for your son?"

"I tried, but he wouldn't listen." They had been over this so many times, and each time he hoped would be the last. "Robert never took to astrology the way Melinda did. He wasn't so much a non-believer, he just ignored it. It was his nature to be rebellious, and maybe that was just another way of displaying it." He took his arm back and turned his collar up. They walked again, disconnected. "I knew the transits and progressions Robert was facing and warned him repeatedly to avoid dangerous situations. But it's exactly under such aspects that one would find himself in the position he did. He saved the life of the bodega owner."

She nodded. "At the cost of his own."

"Don't you know that I would gladly give my own life in return for his?"

The tears started to fall from her eyes. She nodded. "Yes, I do know."

She took his arm again and held on so tightly it hurt. But it was a good hurt. She took out a tissue from her coat pocket and dabbed at her eyes, then shook a little and regained control. They walked for another half hour. The effects of the wine began to wane. "Let's go home and build a fire."

They walked back to the dark house. As they reached the porch Lowell thought he heard footsteps behind them. He turned quickly, just catching the glimpse of someone scurrying into the woods. *Probably some teenagers looking for a make-out spot.* He thought. But for some reason it left him feeling uneasy.

Lowell went in first and turned on the porch light. "I guess Melinda's still on her date."

"Are you being a jealous father?" Catherine chuckled.

"No. Actually I'm glad she's out. I don't think she dates much."

"You see her all the time, don't you know?"

He shook his head. "We don't discuss certain things."

"Why David Lowell, you've become such a prude. Whatever happened to the fiery, sizzling lover who used to take me into these very same woods and make love to me under the stars?"

"Please, Catherine, the chipmunks are blushing."

They went into the living room, a large space with very high ceilings and exposed wooden beams. The house was built in the early twentieth century and had an old, solid feeling about it, a structure from a different era, before houses were made of metal and looked like they belonged in a Picasso painting.

The fireplace was huge and had originally been used to heat this part of the house before the oil furnace was installed. David took some kindling and laid it across the base of the fireplace. Then he took four large logs and arranged them in such a way as to maximize the starter fire of the kindling and make sure they all caught the blaze. There was always at least a cord of wood stacked in the backyard, and before he settled down, David made several trips to ensure enough wood to last the evening.

They sat on the floor and watched as the wood crackled and sang. "Do you think we should have a nightcap?"

Catherine thought for a moment. "I'm pretty sober now. I think a cognac wouldn't hurt, do you?"

He went to the bar to the left of the fireplace, took two snifters, and poured them each a Remy. Then he sat back down on the floor and handed one to Catherine.

They clicked their glasses and each took a sip. The hot liquid drizzling down his throat had a relaxing, soothing effect.

"You know," he said, "I almost never drink this stuff. I only seem to like cognac by a blazing fire. They seem to go together in some strange way."

She took a sip and looked at her ex-husband, the firelight dancing a minuet behind him. There was something so right about this man, and yet…She sighed. Then took another sip. She was careful, didn't want to get sloppy. She had been drinking quite a bit lately and was a little concerned about it. She didn't want this to turn into a fight, as it had the last time they were together. "David," he turned toward her. "David I…"

"What is it, Catherine?"

"Why don't you stay until Monday morning?"

"Okay."

She sipped her Remy. "In the guest room."

He sighed. "Whatever makes you comfortable."

Melinda got home about midnight and found her parents asleep under a blue blanket, in front of a dying fire. Rather than wake them, she built the fire up again, made sure it was secured behind the metal guard, and went to sleep.

◇◇◇

They all had breakfast together the next morning and spent the day meandering through town. Zack joined them for lunch at a local diner and they reminisced. The evening was a quiet dinner at home just for the family. They built another fire and played Clue. David won.

Chapter Fifteen

The ride home was subdued and thoughtful. Melinda fell asleep. When they got on the New York State Thruway, Andy buzzed.

Lowell was in a quiet funk. He picked up the car phone. "What's up?"

"I think we've got a tail."

Lowell perked up. "Really?"

"I don't know. Let me watch 'em for a few minutes."

Lowell lowered the partition window between the front and back of the limo so he could talk to Andy directly. "Which car?"

Andy pulled into the right lane and slowed the limo down. He pointed to a blue sedan as it passed them on the left. "I noticed it several times in Woodstock, and they left just as we did."

They watched as the car put on its blinker and pulled into their lane a few cars ahead of them, getting off the highway at the next exit. They couldn't see the license plate.

Andy shrugged. "I guess I was wrong."

"Maybe, but he may have realized he was made and got off to avoid suspicion. But who would be following us?"

Melinda stirred. The talking awakened her. "Who's following us?"

Lowell looked at his daughter curled up in a little ball, looking about ten. "Nobody, honey, go back to sleep."

She did.

They got back to the city at three in the afternoon. Andy dropped David at the office and then took Melinda downtown to her office.

Lowell spent the rest of the day reviewing the information he already had and putting his mind back on track. At five Sarah came in. "I'm heading home. You need anything before I go?"

"No. But I'm leaving too. If you wait a minute I'll walk you out."

They exited the building and turned left. Although it was still quite warm there was a sharp late summer breeze. Sarah pulled her shirt collar up around her ears. "I could use a drink."

Lowell looked at his watch. "Me too. Let's go to Morgan's Pub. I'll buy you a cocktail."

"Okay, sailor. But don't get fresh." Sarah winked.

They sat at the bar in Morgan's Pub, a well-known neighborhood saloon with a decidedly upscale menu. Lowell was very fussy about where he ate and drank. In his youth he had worked for several years as a bartender in Manhattan and knew the truth. Most bars weren't very clean. And bartenders who wash their glasses in the sink behind the bar with the little twirling washing machine didn't clean them at all. The water was never hot enough and the brushes were often filthy. Morgan's gave the impression of being a rundown dive, but Lowell knew that was an illusion to please the bohemian fantasies of the middle-class clientele. The food was top-notch, the staff knowledgeable and affable, and the glasses all went back to the kitchen to be washed.

Sarah's martini glass looked huge. She held it with both hands. "What made you study aikido?"

"I'm not a large man, as you know. As a child I had to fend off bullies and stand my ground." Lowell took a sip of his Beck's. "I took karate and became efficient at it, but it almost tore my tendons to shreds and I was always in pain. It takes a great toll on the body, especially the legs. Most karate aficionados are half crippled by the time they're fifty, and the truth is, unless you're a real master at it, it can actually be counterproductive. I did earn a brown belt."

Sarah toothpicked an olive from her martini and nibbled at it. "Isn't that right before a black belt?"

"Yes. Anyway, I knew a guy when I was studying in Boston who was a black belt. He was quite good at it, and usually won the sparring contests. One night he was in a bar and a couple of big guys got fresh with his date. He went outside with them where they clobbered him. Apparently they were also into the martial arts. Put him in the hospital for a month with a broken jaw and some cracked ribs. Had he not been over-confident he might have left the bar without incident, or maybe sought backup."

"So you took up aikido?"

"It's a much gentler and less intrusive form of self-defense. Of course I try to use all of the knowledge I've accrued from judo, karate, aikido, and common sense, if I get into a physical altercation. And I also use whatever is available to me at the time."

"I remember how you used the fruit as weapons down in Soho in the rock 'n' roll case."

He nodded. "Anything can be used as a weapon. You read *Shibumi*. So you understand the philosophy."

She sipped her drink and nodded. "How does aikido work?"

"It has to do with pressure points, direction, and position more than actual strength. For example, the body bends in certain ways." He held up his left hand. "The wrist will bend forward quite well, but has less mobility backwards. And if you try to bend it from side to side, there is almost no give. If I can get your wrist into a position where I can manipulate its motion, I can cause you great pain and even a broken bone using very little power. The same is true of all the joints. Anyone can learn the technique, with a little work."

"Can you show me something now?"

It was still early and the bar was fairly empty. A couple were sipping martinis, a few patrons were watching football. The bartender was at the service bar at the other end of the room chatting with the blond twenty-something waitress.

"Here, stand up and I'll show you a simple move." She stood. "Grab my right wrist with your right hand."

She did so. Then Lowell placed his left hand on top of hers holding it in place, twisted his right hand inward around her wrist, and put just the slightest amount of pressure on it. She went to her knees.

"Ow!"

"Sorry, but that was the least amount of pressure I could use. If I had used enough I would have broken your wrist."

"And it doesn't matter who's stronger?"

"Up to a point. A giant of a man would not easily succumb to something like that. But yes, size is less important than angle, and the proper training."

"Can I try it on you?"

He sighed. "If you must."

He grabbed her right wrist with his right hand. She thought for a moment, and then put her left hand on his holding it tight as he had done, twisted her right hand around, and put pressure down, causing Lowell to drop to one knee.

"Okay, not bad for a first time. You can let go now."

She released the hold. "Wow, cool!"

"Once you have your adversary in a weakened position you must then finish the job with a properly placed punch or kick. Otherwise when he gets up he'll resume the attack more guardedly."

He took a sip of his beer.

"Show me more."

"Sarah."

"Pleeeese?"

He smirked and shook his head. "Okay. Here's another simple trick. Put your hands on my chest as if you're going to push me back."

They both stood up and Sarah put her hands against his chest. Lowell held his forearms against her hands holding them in place, then leaned forward, bending her wrists backwards just slightly.

Sarah's eyes opened wide. "Wow."

"Now you try it."

They reversed the actions and she got it on the first try.

"Holy crap, Batman! Teach me more."

"Later. I came here to relax."

They sipped their drinks and chatted about the caseload. The bar was beginning to fill up with weary mid-town workers unwinding after a long day.

Sarah pushed her bright red hair back behind her ears. "That Williamson thing was easy enough."

"Hmm, yes I suppose so."

"Well you did find the child in time."

Lowell tugged on his ponytail. "I hope so."

"But something is still bothering you."

Lowell looked her in the eye but said nothing.

Chapter Sixteen

They finished their drinks and left the bar.

"Will you walk me home?"

He patted her hand in a fatherly fashion. "Of course."

She took his arm and they walked west across Twenty-fourth Street. When they reached Seventh Avenue they turned south.

The late August breeze had chilled. Sarah shivered slightly. "Do you mind if I ask you something personal?"

"When have I ever minded?" He laughed. "And when have you ever hesitated? You are an Aries, after all. What is it?"

"How did you live with the loss of Robert?"

"One day at a time."

"I'm sorry, I shouldn't have asked you."

He put his arm around her shoulder. "It's okay, Sarah. You're family now. You can ask me anything you want to. At first it was unbearable. I couldn't sleep or stop thinking about it. But as the months passed it became a part of me, almost as if Robert still lived in my ongoing memories and had never died. I would think about how he would respond to a situation and often found myself talking to him as if he were there with me."

Sarah grabbed his arm tighter. "Your marriage…"

Lowell breathed in deeply. "For a long time Catherine blamed me for Robert's death as I think you already know. It became too painful for us to be together. He was always there between us. But as the months turned into years it receded a bit into the background."

"But you didn't forget him."

He shook his head. "Not a day goes by that I don't think of him and wish he were here living out the life I know he could have created for himself. But I also finally understood that it was doing nobody any good to wallow in the sadness. Robert wouldn't have wanted that."

"That's why you became a detective."

"You think so?"

"I think you had to direct your anger and feelings of impotence into something useful, and helping those who had no other place to turn seemed like a way to do so."

He smiled.

They were walking down Eleventh Street toward Fifth Avenue when two men approached them.

One of the men had a long scar on the side of his face that appeared to be fairly old. He stopped in front of them.

Lowell was not easily intimidated, but his concern for Sarah's safety limited his choices. "Can I help you?"

The other man nodded silently and took out a gun.

Sarah's body tensed.

The gunman pointed to a double-parked blue Chevy. It looked like the same car Lowell had seen on the highway, but he couldn't be sure. "Get in the car."

Lowell took a deep breath to center himself. "Now why would we want to do that?"

"You want to die?" The man pointed the pistol at Lowell and turned to his partner. "Grab the girl."

The scarred man reached out and took hold of Sarah's right wrist. She had only a second to react. She reached over with her left hand, tightly held on to the man's hand, and twisted her right hand around, just as Lowell had taught her. Then with all of her might she pushed down on his wrist. The man went to his knees, and before he could regain his footing Sarah stepped back and kicked him in the groin with her pointed boot. He went down on the sidewalk, grabbing himself in agony.

"Ow, you bitch!"

He lay there moaning and rolling around.

As the other man was distracted, Lowell grabbed the hand holding the gun, stepping out of the way of the barrel, just as two shots rang out. The bullets flew past him, one landing into the side of a brownstone, the other going through the windshield of a white Mazda and setting off the car's alarm.

Lowell twisted the gun from the man's hand and threw it into the street. Then he pulled the assailant toward him and simultaneously slammed the man's chest with an open hand, pushing him backwards onto the ground. He kicked the man in the face, and blood oozed from his mouth. Lowell grabbed Sarah's hand and they ran down the street.

When they were a few blocks away Sarah was still trying to catch her breath.

Lowell looked back, but nobody was following. He turned to her. "Are you alright?"

She was breathing heavily, but smiling. "That was the most amazing thing I've ever done!" She raised her fist. "Women rule!"

"Come on, Wonder Woman, let's get home." He took out his cell phone and a few minutes later Andy was there.

"What happened, Boss?"

"We were attacked by two men who tried to push us into a blue sedan."

Andy nodded. "Same car from the highway?"

"I'm not sure," said Lowell. "But it would be some coincidence if not. We're going to have to watch our backs now."

Andy unconsciously touched the shoulder holster that held his revolver. "I'm ready."

They dropped Sarah off at her building near the corner of Sixth Avenue. Lowell walked her to her front stoop. "Will you be alright alone tonight?"

Sarah's eyes opened wide. "Why? You don't think I'm in any danger, do you?"

"No, I just want to be careful."

"I'll be fine. The building is secure and the super lives right next to me." She grinned. "He knows karate."

"Get a good night's sleep. I'm going to need you sharp and alert tomorrow." He watched as she climbed the half dozen steps to her front door.

She waved and entered her foyer. Lowell entered the limo and waited for a few minutes eyeing the streets, and then Andy drove him to the townhouse.

Chapter Seventeen

Roland looked haggard. "So you were attacked by two strangers last night?"

Lowell and Sarah were in Lieutenant Roland's office at the Nineteenth Precinct. His desk was inundated with piles of papers and haphazardly scattered folders. On the wall behind his chair were framed pictures of Ronald Reagan and George H. Bush. "W's" portrait was noticeably missing. Roland held a cup of coffee with two hands and intermittently blew on it and took small sips.

Roland looked at Sarah. "This isn't the first time I'm giving you this advice…"

"I know Lieutenant," she interrupted, "I should find another line of work."

Roland shook his head. "If you were my daughter…" He shrugged. "Would you both mind looking through some mug shots?"

"Not at all," said Lowell.

They went downstairs and started what Lowell knew was often a fruitless search through the pictures of known criminals.

After almost two hours, Roland came in.

"Anything?"

Lowell shook his head. He stood up and stretched, looked at the time on his phone, and was about to tell Sarah to stop when she shouted.

"That's him! That's the guy I kicked in the...street." She giggled. Lowell was afraid she was going to raise her arm and shout triumphantly.

Roland stood behind her and looked at the face. "Are you sure? I mean absolutely sure?"

Sarah nodded emphatically.

"I'll never forget the look on his face when he doubled over." She looked down at the picture. "Call me a bitch, will ya?"

Roland picked up the phone and pushed a few buttons. "Harry, it's Phil. I just got a positive ID on George McFarley... Yes, I'm pretty sure it's accurate...I don't know what he's doing in New York...He wasn't alone. He had some bozo with him. I want a list of known associates ASAP." He hung up.

Lowell retied his ponytail, and looked Roland squarely in the face. "What is it? What's bothering you?"

Roland looked at Sarah, shook his head, and then looked away.

Sarah caught the look. "It's okay, Lieutenant, I'm a big girl. What is it?"

He looked back at her, and then looked at Lowell. "Okay, I don't know who you pissed off, but this is bad business. This guy's murder-for-hire. And he seems to really like his work. He's accused of chopping up several people, at least one while she was still alive."

Sarah stood up. "What? I'm not that big a girl. Oh my God!"

"Phil, are you sure?"

Roland stood and stretched. "David, this isn't something I would joke about. This guy's a nut job. But he's very smart. And very elusive, and there's no evidence to connect him to any of the murders he's suspected of. We try to keep tabs on his whereabouts, but it's difficult. He falls off the radar for long periods of time. This is the first lead we've had on him in months. What are you working on that would bring up such a headache?"

"I'm looking into a pretty large embezzlement, and I just finished a missing person case, and a few other odds and ends. But I can't imagine any of them would lead to this."

"How big an embezzlement?"

"Millions."

Roland whistled. "That must have been some paper bag."

Lowell chuckled. "Not that kind of embezzlement. It was a retirement fund for a company. The money was transferred electronically, probably to a dummy account."

"Well, that's enough money for someone to make sure you don't get too close. Do you know who's responsible?"

"I just figured out who stole the money and told the president of the company a few days ago."

"And you were attacked last night? I'd look into it if I were you."

Lowell nodded. "Yes. I plan to."

Sarah didn't look so good.

"Are you alright?" asked the policeman.

She nodded slightly. "I'll be fine in a few minutes." Her pallor was a pale and her eyes glassy.

Roland's phone rang.

"Roland…Yes, Captain, I've got two witnesses…David Lowell and Sarah Palmer…Yes *that* David Lowell…Okay, I'll tell them."

He hung up.

"Well?" Lowell's concern was obvious.

"The captain wants you to be careful."

"I have every intention of staying alive, Lieutenant. But thank him for his concern."

"You still have that big guy on your payroll?"

"Yes, Andy still works for me."

"Well, use him. Don't be stubborn."

Roland's phone rang again. He picked it up, and then waved them off.

Lowell and Sarah got up and left without saying goodbye.

Chapter Eighteen

Melinda and Mort were in Lowell's office watching him pace in front of the windows.

Melinda was seated at his desk, a worried look on her face. "What cases are you working on?"

Lowell stopped to pet Keaton. "Nothing that I thought would put us in danger."

"Well, someone wants you out of the way."

He nodded. "I think we have to go into protective mode."

Mort's eyes opened wide. "You're not going to make us stay at the townhouse again, are you?"

"I don't think that's quite necessary. But I won't take any chances with our safety. We're going to have to flush this problem out into the open."

"Okay," said Mort. "What's next on the agenda?"

"We have to shake up these two cases and see what falls out." Lowell buzzed Sarah.

"Yes, Boss?"

"Get me the marshmallow guy."

Sarah broke up laughing.

"Sarah!"

"Sorry, Boss, I'm just a little nervous. My life might be in danger because of a marshmallow man. Boy, if I ever write a book…"

She hung up.

Lowell's phone rang. "This is Lowell."

"It's Buddy. Have you got something for me, Mr. Lowell?" His voice was animated and cheerful. One could hear the smile in every word.

"Are your phones lines secure?"

"Mr. Lowell, we're a candy company, not the CIA. We run an informal business here. I guess someone could listen in on a conversation. Why do you ask?"

"I have some things to discuss with you. I think it would be best to do so in person. Do you have time to see me today?"

"Why, sure. You can come over any time. I'm always here."

"My associate and I will be there in an hour. In the meantime would you please not discuss this business with anyone?"

"Yes sir, I'll try. By the way, do you like marshmallows? I can send you up a nice mixed selection of our top sellers, if you like?"

Lowell was about to refuse when he thought of his team. "You know what, why don't you. I'm a vegetarian so I can't eat them. But my staff might enjoy them. I'll put Sarah back on and she'll give you an address. Thank you."

"It's my pleasure. Looking forward to seeing you."

Lowell switched to the intercom. "Sarah, please give Mr. Ferguson our mailing address and then come in here."

A few moments later Sarah entered. "So what's up, Boss?"

The astrologer looked at his staff. "I'm not sure what's going on, but I want you all to be extremely careful. Things aren't quite as they seem, and I appear to be a target once again. I take this very seriously. Andy will always be a phone call away. Don't hesitate to call him or me if you see something funny, or if you just don't feel quite right."

"Dad, do you think we're in any real danger?"

"I don't think so. If anyone is at risk I assume it would be me. But I'm not taking any unnecessary chances, nor should any of you. Take extra precautions and stay alert."

They all nodded.

Lowell got up. "Mort and I are going to see our client and try to figure this all out."

Chapter Nineteen

Andy drove Lowell and Mort to the Lower East Side. They entered a gray stone building about one hundred years old, and a rickety ancient elevator with a metal door that had to be closed manually. On the third floor the elevator doors opened to the offices of The Happy Snappy Marshmallow Company.

A huge plastic effigy of a smiling Marshmallow Man stood next to the reception desk. Mort couldn't resist pushing his finger into the statue, which was made of a rubbery substance. His finger went in a good two inches.

They approach the smiling receptionist. A plastic Ziploc container filled with various colored marshmallows sat on her desk.

"David Lowell to see…"

"Yes, Mr. Lowell," her smile widened, "Buddy is expecting you. Just go down the hall to the last door on your left."

Apparently everyone did call him Buddy, even his employees.

They walked down the hall past framed pictures of multi-colored marshmallows, giant S'mores, and children sitting around a campfire with marshmallow laden sticks. They passed half a dozen employees, all smiling, and all quite overweight. They must've liked the product.

The door to Buddy's office was open. He was sitting behind his desk. Lowell knocked on the door frame.

Buddy looked up, a huge smile on his face. "Mr. Lowell, please come in." He stood and extended his hand.

Lowell shook it. "This is my associate Mort Simpson."

"How do you do, Mr. Simpson?"

"Call me Mort."

They shook hands, and then they all sat.

Buddy was a short, squat, squishy man. He looked amazingly like the figurine out front, and Lowell wondered if he had been the model for the company's icon, or if was just coincidence.

Buddy opened a plastic container that was sitting on his desk. It was filled with various varieties of the sweet treats. "Please, help yourself."

Mort took a coconut covered one and popped it into his mouth.

"Now, what can I do for you gentlemen?"

"Have you contacted the FBI yet?" asked Lowell.

"Just spoke to them yesterday." His voice was cheery, the smile firmly planted on his face. "The agent I spoke with, Bill Jensen, was less than encouraging. He said the evidence was shabby at best. But I insisted, pointing out the gravity of the situation. He said he'd think about it."

"I might have a chat with Agent Jensen." Lowell tugged on his ponytail. "Buddy, did you tell anyone about what we talked about?"

There was silence for a few moments. "Well, I told my partner, but I don't think he told anyone."

"Can you find out?"

"Sure. I'll get him in here right now and you can ask him yourself." He picked up the phone and pushed a few numbers. "Ralph, would you mind coming into my office for a few moments? Thank you." He hung up. "Do you mind if I ask what this is all about?"

Lowell considered the question before answering. "There's been some trouble and I need to discover its origin."

Buddy took a chocolate-covered marshmallow and ate it. "Trouble, what kind of trouble?"

"My assistant Sarah and I were attacked the other night."

Buddy looked absolutely horrified, the smile gone. "Attacked? Oh my goodness. I hope you're both alright."

"Yes, we're fine. We managed to dissuade the assailants."

"Well, thank God for that." The smile returned. "Are you sure it has to do with our business?"

"No, I'm not. That's why we're here today, to try and uncover the source of the problem."

There was a light tapping on the door. Buddy waved his hand. "Ralph, come in. I want you to meet David Lowell, the detective I told you about, and his associate, Mort Simpson."

A tall, extremely thin man entered. He was not smiling. "How do you do? I understand from Buddy that you've got a lead on our missing money."

His voice was loud and high-pitched. Lowell wondered if there were any secrets at all in this company.

"Do you mind if we close the door?" asked the detective.

Buddy frowned. "Well, I suppose not."

Ralph closed the door behind him, walked over to the desk and stood next to Buddy. They reminded Lowell of Abbott and Costello. Mort and Lowell exchanged a quick glance.

"This is my partner and brother-in-law, Ralph Murphy." Buddy ate another marshmallow. "Apparently Mr. Lowell was attacked a few nights ago."

Ralph looked appalled. "Attacked? Well, Mr. Lowell, what does this have to do with us? We're a family business."

"Yes," said Lowell, "a family business with a multimillion dollar thief. Have you discussed the situation with anyone?"

The skinny man replied. "Well, not directly."

"What do you mean?"

"It's hard to keep things quiet around here."

Lowell shook his head. "I don't doubt it."

"I mean, people overhear things, you know?"

"And who do you think overheard you?"

Ralph looked thoughtful. "I guess everyone. We don't have secrets at Happy Snappy."

Lowell nodded. "I think you should start considering it."

Buddy ate a green one. "You don't think one of our people attacked you, do you?"

"Not directly. But apparently someone was paid to have me silenced, and until I'm sure who it was I must look at all possibilities. We're dealing with the theft of a great deal of money. If the thieves are caught they will face a very long prison sentence. That's motivation enough for someone to do almost anything to prevent our succeeding."

Ralph nodded. "Well, I did overhear our receptionist, Martha, talking about what's been happening on the phone to her boyfriend."

Buddy looked pale. "Why didn't you mention it?"

"I didn't think it was important. I mean, by now everyone knows that something is up. But I don't believe anyone knows exactly what."

"No," said Lowell, "nobody except the person who stole it."

"Ralph," said Buddy, "they think it was Harriet."

"Harriet? Oh my God, no. But she's such a competent bookkeeper."

Lowell nodded. "Yes, it takes a lot of competence to successfully steal millions of dollars."

Both partners nodded.

"But how could she do it?" asked Ralph.

Buddy reached for another treat, but Ralph grabbed his wrist and stared at him. Buddy put the top back on the container. "They believe her brother was in on it. That he used his office in the bank to move the money." He turned to Lowell. "Is that about right?"

Lowell nodded. "That's why I insisted that you bring the FBI in. They need to audit the bank's records, and quickly, before the money can be moved. That's the only way we will know for sure."

Buddy unconsciously reached for another sweet treat, but caught Ralph looking at him and he pulled his hand away.

Lowell stood. "Please let me know what the FBI finds out. And in the meantime I must ask you both to be discrete and not talk about this around the office."

Buddy stood up and shook hands with Lowell and Mort. "I'll let you know the moment I hear anything. This is terrible business, just terrible." He reached over and grabbed a red, white, and blue marshmallow before Ralph could react. "These are left over from the Fourth of July. Vanilla, blueberry, and strawberry. They're very popular. I'll send some in your order."

He popped it in his mouth.

In the elevator Mort turned to Lowell. "What did you think?"

Lowell pulled on his ponytail. "I thought marshmallows weren't very fattening."

Mort giggled. "I guess if you eat enough of anything…"

Chapter Twenty

That night Lowell was having an early dinner alone at Louie's on Twenty-fifth Street. He was being extra cautious and had sent the staff home early with Andy. After a hearty vegetarian stew and a glass of organic Merlot he paid his bill and headed home. The long walk would help his digestion, and Andy was only a phone call away. It was almost seven. Rush hour had winded down and the traffic was moving along quickly.

He began walking uptown on First Avenue when he saw two men approach a yellow Toyota stopped at a light. One went around to the passenger's side and opened the door. The other yanked the driver's door open and began pulling a middle-aged woman out by her hair.

Lowell ran across the street and was a few feet from the car when a short young woman joined him.

"You take the one on the driver's side, if you think you can handle it, Grandpa."

"Grandpa? Listen, young lady, why don't you just go about your business and let me deal with this?" He turned to look at her and was startled. He had noticed her earlier that day, half a block behind him looking in store windows, and had begun to wonder if perhaps she was tailing him.

She ignored his advice and ran around to the passenger's side.

He ran to the driver's side, grabbed the assailant's arm at the elbow and pushed against the joint, causing that man great pain. The man let the woman's head go and turned his attention toward Lowell.

"Want a piece of me, asshole, you got it."

He swung a slow, wide, left hook, which David was able to step away from. The force of the punch upset the man's balance, and David pulled him forward while putting his leg out. The man tripped over it and fell facedown on the ground. David walked over and took the man's arm at the shoulder and twisted it, dislocating the joint. The man screamed in pain and then passed out.

Lowell turned toward the second assailant just in time to witness the young woman who had joined in the rescue execute a perfect judo shoulder-throw, tossing the man on his back. As he lifted his head she swung her left foot whacking him on the side of his head and knocking him out.

She looked at the man lying at Lowell's feet. "Not bad, Grandpa."

"If you call me grandpa one more time I'm going to take you over my knee and spank the living daylights out of you."

"Oh, do you promise? Fifty shades of gray." She laughed. "Anyway, lighten up, I meant it as a compliment. I like older men. Takes guys a long time to grow up."

A cop car pulled over behind them and two of New York's finest exited.

"What's going on here?" asked a young officer.

The driver of the car came over. "Officer, those two men were trying to pull me out of my car when this man and woman came to my rescue."

"I see."

Lowell presented his card. "David Lowell."

The officer looked down at it. "Okay, Mr. Lowell, if you wouldn't mind giving us a brief statement."

After they both had told their tale to the officer, Lowell headed uptown once again. The young woman walked right next to him, keeping pace. She was a few inches shorter than Lowell's five-feet-eight.

"Young lady, what do you want? And why have you been following me?"

"Oh you notice, huh? I never was good at tailing. It's just as well. I want to talk to you."

She reached into the pocket of her jeans and pulled out a small, well-worn leather wallet. She flipped it open. "Officer Karen Sweeney," then she flipped it closed and returned it to her pocket.

"That wasn't a New York badge, was it?"

"LAPD."

"Hmm. What does the LAPD want with me?"

"We're pursuing someone in New York and your name came up."

"Who are you chasing?"

"Williamson."

Lowell stopped walking and turned toward her. "Dr. Williamson?"

She nodded. "I was tailing him too and saw him go to your office. What did Williamson want with you?"

"I wouldn't stay in business very long if I betrayed the confidence of my clients, would I?"

"Well, it doesn't matter. I'm not leaving until I find out." They walked uptown together at a New York pace Lowell was used to. "Hey, could you slow down just a bit? I got short legs."

"Can't keep up with the old guy?"

She smiled. "Maybe not on foot. Anyway, I was told to look you up and I was going to introduce myself eventually. I just wanted to check you out on the sly for a little while, see who I was dealing with."

"Told to look me up by whom?"

"You know a detective in L.A. named Samuels?"

"Wally?"

She nodded. "He told me to introduce myself while in New York. Said you were old friends."

"Let me see that badge again."

She took it out. "What's the matter, don't you trust me?"

"For forty bucks you could have a phony made up. You have any other ID?"

She laughed. "You're Wally's friend, alright. Here," she reached into her back pocket and took out her personal wallet.

Lowell looked through it and found a picture of the woman in uniform standing next to Wally Samuels. It looked like a Christmas party at the precinct. Satisfied, he returned it to her.

"So what can I do for you?"

"Private detective from L.A. named Mickey Broad was found shot to death in his apartment in Venice, California, and I'd like to know who killed him. He was in New York shortly before his murder. I believe the doctor was his last client. I find him to be a person of interest in the case."

Lowell nodded. "Williamson mentioned hiring a PI in California. So what do you want from me?"

"I want to hire you. I need to know what he told you. I can pay you five hundred bucks. That's all I've got." She took a check from her wallet already made out to Lowell for that amount. "Only don't cash it until I get back to L.A."

"Officer…"

"Sweeney."

"Officer Sweeney, I have no intention of giving you any information regarding my client or his case."

"I was hoping in the spirit of cooperation with law enforcement…"

"I tell you what, any information that I feel isn't crossing the line I will share with you. How's that?"

He started to walk rapidly. She struggled to keep up.

"I take it that walking is not a sport in L.A. like it is in New York?"

"We only walk on treadmills."

"Well," said Lowell, "get used to it. But don't expect to get much information."

"Like I said before, I'm not leaving your side until I find out a few things."

"Where are you staying?"

"Wally sort of thought you might be willing to put me up for a few nights. He said you have a big place. And I wouldn't get in the way."

"Why don't you just stay in a hotel and charge it to the LAPD?"

She shrugged.

"You're out here on your own, aren't you? Does your boss even know what you're up to?"

"He thinks I'm on vacation visiting my aunt in Greenwich, Connecticut." She laughed. "He'd bust a gut if he knew."

"Look," said the detective, "I don't mind helping you out a bit while you're in town, but I'm a very private person and I don't really like house guests."

"You won't even know I'm there, I promise. I'll be as quiet as a mouse and won't leave my room."

"I don't think so."

Karen stopped walking and gently grabbed Lowell's arm. He stopped too. "I wouldn't ask, except that, well, I'm kinda broke right now and it took all my dough to get here. I really don't have enough for a hotel room."

"Why don't I just pay for a room for you?"

She shook her head, her short brown bangs flip-flopping across her forehead. "I could never take charity, and it would just take too long to pay it back. Besides, I'm hiring you. It wouldn't work if you paid for things. This way if you're ever in L.A. you can call on me to return the favor for anything you needed. You can always stay at my place."

"I don't think so."

"Please? Just think about it, okay? You won't regret it, I promise. Do you live around here?"

"No. I live uptown off of Lexington Avenue, in Carnegie Hill."

"Don't know where that is. This is my first trip to New York since I was twelve. Come on, I'll drive you home. The car's down this street."

They turned down Twenty-fifth Street toward Second Avenue. "Why do you have a car in New York?"

"How else was I supposed to get here?"

"You mean you drove from L.A.?" Lowell was incredulous.

"Yeah. It's not so bad when you got company. Here's my car."

"Company? What company?"

They were stopped next to an old, beat-up, gray Toyota, vintage 2000 or so. Karen opened the door with a key and clicked the lock-release on the driver's door. "Get in."

Lowell walked around to the passenger's door and opened it. It squeaked from rust and old age. He stuck his head into the car and his face was immediately slobbered on by the largest, black dog he had ever seen. "What the hell?"

"That's Luigi. He won't bother you. Just push him into the backseat. He's a pussy cat, really." She got into the driver's seat and grabbed the dog by the collar. "Go on, you big baby, get in the back. That's a good boy." She looked out the passenger door. "You can get in now."

Lowell was wiping his face with a handkerchief as he got in the car. "What do you intend to do with him?"

"What do you mean? He's staying with me. I wouldn't leave my buddy for all the money in the world." She looked at him sheepishly. "Nobody's going to let me stay in a hotel with him. Now do you get it? What do you say?"

"You've been here for a few days already, haven't you? Where have you been staying?"

She waved her hand around the Toyota. "Welcome to Chez Sweeney."

"You've been living in your car?"

"Yep. But I got Luigi for protection."

Lowell was used to being alone, especially since his divorce. He had guests infrequently, though on one occasion he had to house his entire staff at his townhouse during a particularly dangerous case. But he really didn't like being around people that much, especially strangers. And while on a case he preferred to stay in his office. But he wouldn't allow a stranger to stay in his townhouse without his presence, which meant that he would also have to stay at the townhouse. But this woman was Wally's friend. He couldn't let her sleep in the car. And he did have one serious weakness—animals. He loved them all unconditionally. This was the main reason he was a vegetarian. He looked at the monster in the backseat, its sad eyes watching his every move, as if he knew Lowell controlled his future.

He sighed and nodded reluctantly. "Alright. For a few days. Why are you doing this and risking so much?"

"The detective that was killed?"

"Broad."

She nodded. "My name is Karen Broad Sweeney. He was my mother's brother and my favorite relative. And I loved him very much."

Chapter Twenty-one

"What makes you think Williamson had anything to do with your uncle's death?"

Karen was sitting on the couch in the living room of Lowell's townhouse, Luigi asleep at her feet. "I don't know. I'm just following the trail. The last time I spoke to him he told me that he had discovered something strange about a case he was working on and he needed to follow it up."

"He didn't tell you what he found out?"

She shook her head. "I only know that he came to the East Coast for a few days, and then flew back to L.A. I got one short phone message while he was here." She took her cell phone from her pocket, pushed a few buttons, and gave it to Lowell.

He listened. "*Hi Karen, I'm in a hurry, I'll call you later when I have more time.*" There was the sound of rustling papers. "*I've got the weirdest case I've ever had. Things aren't at all what they seem. Listen kid, if anything happens to me I want you to take the keys I gave you last year, go to my N.Y. apartment and get the mail. I sent something to myself and if I can't get there for any reason, you must check it out.*" He could hear a door opening. "*I gotta go. I'll call you soon,*" said in a whisper. Then the message ended.

Lowell handed her the phone. "Doesn't tell us much. Not even if it was Williamson he was talking about. Maybe he was looking into something else altogether."

"That's possible. But I'm going to follow my uncle's footsteps until I find out what happened."

"If Williamson was involved, he lives and works in New Jersey. Why are you in Manhattan?"

"My uncle was born here and grew up on the Lower East Side. He always kept his rent-controlled apartment to use when he was in New York. He held onto it for decades, even after he moved to California, and that's where he was staying when he was here. He went back to L.A. right before I received this message, and he was dead forty-eight hours later. That's all I got to go on. Sometimes all we have is our instincts."

"If your uncle has a place here…"

"Why aren't I staying there?"

Lowell shrugged.

"I went down there and saw the super when I first got here. No dogs allowed. And he was very unbending and nasty about it. He said that if he found a dog living in one of his apartments he'd call the cops immediately. And I think it would be pretty difficult to hide Luigi."

"I see."

Lowell's live-in housekeeper, Julia entered. She was originally from Brazil and went to work for Lowell soon after her husband died, almost seven years before.

"Mr. Lowell, the guest room is ready." She looked down at Luigi, her displeasure quite apparent. "What do you want me to do with him?"

Karen bent down by Luigi, who rolled on his back so she could rub his belly. "Don't worry about him. He's as gentle as a cow."

The housekeeper nodded. "And twice as big. You got food for him?"

"I've got a fifty-pound bag in the car."

"And what are you going to feed him tomorrow?" She turned to leave. "Bring it to me and I'll take care of him."

"I'll do it," said Karen. "After all, he's my dog."

"Oh, no you won't. He may be your dog but it's my house. I'll be in the kitchen if anyone needs me." She went down the hall.

Lowell watched with amusement. "Look, Karen, I'll try to help you find out what happened to your uncle in any way I can. Feel free to ask any of my staff for help as well. I'll let them know tomorrow. But I have to separate your situation from my case. I can't let it interfere with my investigation."

"I understand. I appreciate any help you can lend."

Lowell got up. "I've got some work to do downstairs in my office. Will you be alright here for a while?"

"Sure. I'm real tired anyway. Luigi and I will watch some TV and then turn in early. We haven't had a good night's sleep since we left L.A."

She yawned and tilted her head from side to side, stretching her neck muscles. "I've got some phone calls to make early in the morning. Also, there's a guy in Queens who might know something. Last time I spoke to my uncle he mentioned a name and an address in Queens, New York. Where is that? Queens? And how do I get there?"

"It's that way." Lowell pointed east. "But it's a big borough with lots of different neighborhoods and you don't know your way around. Let me know if you decide to follow up on it. I'll have my driver take you."

"Really? You mean like a chauffeur?"

"Exactly like one. Just call my office a few hours in advance and let Sarah know where you need to go. Andy will pick you up and take you there." He handed her his card.

"Cool."

Chapter Twenty-two

Lowell awoke at five, as he always did. He went into the kitchen and found Julia had left the coffee maker ready to go, as she always did. He pushed the brew button. Then he went to the front door, opened it, and retrieved the *New York Times*. When he returned to the kitchen the smell of fresh coffee permeated the air. He took a mug from the cupboard and poured a cup. He added a spoonful of organic brown sugar, a dollop of milk, and with his coffee and paper in hand, opened the door from the kitchen to the backyard. He was about to close it when Luigi appeared. He looked up at Lowell with his seemingly sad eyes.

"You've got to be walked, don't you? Okay, big guy. Come on. Where's your mommy? Still asleep upstairs, I'll bet."

He grabbed several plastic bags from under the sink, took the leash that was hanging on the front doorknob, and hooked it up to the dog's collar. Then he took Luigi out and they trotted up Ninety-third Street. When he was done with his business they went back into the townhouse. Lowell picked up his coffee cup and headed toward the backyard, Luigi at his heels.

"You want to come outside?"

Luigi seemed to grin.

Lowell opened the screen door and Luigi plodded down the porch steps. He sniffed around the tiny property marking his territory on the wooden panels.

Lowell put his coffee on the table and sat smiling. "You'd better not let Julia see you do that." His love of animals was absolute. They could do no wrong. He always tried not to place human restrictions or expectations on his four-legged friends, as so many did. *'Never get mad at a dog for being a dog,'* he was fond of saying.

When Luigi was done he walked over and lay down with his head on Lowell's feet. Lowell unconsciously leaned over and rubbed his gigantic head. "You are a sweet thing, aren't you?"

He opened the *Times* and began catching up on the world's events. The front page showed a horrific sight he would probably never forget. It was the carcasses of hundreds of elephants slaughtered in the most barbaric ways with their tusks sliced from their bodies. He read the story, his heart racing, his anger swelling up inside. Armed militia, some backed by the governments of small African nations, were using automatic weapons and even grenades to kill these magnificent beasts. The demand for ivory, especially in China with its newly expanded upper and middle classes, had grown to insane proportions. In one nation the elephant herds which had once numbered in the tens of thousands were down to about 500. There had been no pups born for several years, the fear and understanding of what was happening to them took away even the desire to procreate. Elephants, he knew, were highly intelligent creatures who mourned their dead. This once magnificent herd was mourning their own extinction.

He shook his head, put the paper down, and leaned over to rub Luigi's belly, as if some contact with the animal world could alleviate at least a tiny bit of his disgust at his own species. The dog rolled over onto his back, his tongue hanging from the side of his mouth, a smile on his face.

Julia came out of the house. "I'm making breakfast for you, Mr. Lowell."

"No thank you, Julia. Coffee is all I really want. And how many times have I told you to call me David?"

"Yes sir, Mr. L…David."

"That's better."

"They say that breakfast is the most important meal of the day. I've got eggs and toast cooking. I'll bring it out in a few minutes."

"I really don't…"

"I'll bring it out in a few minutes." Her determination was unbendable.

Lowell sighed. "Alright, I guess a small breakfast won't kill me."

She went back into the house. He went back to the *Times.*

Luigi was bored. He began roaming the tiny estate, sniffing everything. Lowell paid him no mind. He was reading the op-ed page when Julia came out with his meal. Two hard-boiled free-range eggs, multi-grain toast, and jam. She placed the tray on the table.

"This looks wonderful, Julia. Thank you."

"More coffee?"

Lowell looked at his cup, almost empty. "Yes, I could use another."

She went back inside briefly and returned with a silver pot. She poured some into his cup and left the pot on the table. She turned to go back inside, but something caught her eye.

"What are you doing!" she shouted.

Lowell turned his head and saw what she was looking at. Luigi was digging a hole.

"My rhododendrons. My beautiful rhododendrons. Why, you monster."

Luigi picked his head up and looked at her, then looked back at the hole. He lay down prostrate, face to the ground, with his front legs stretched out in front of him, a look of chagrin on his mug.

Julia's face was flush. "You wait here, you, you dog you."

Luigi looked up at Lowell.

He shook his head. "Nothing I can do for you, big guy. You're on your own."

Julia went inside and returned with a broom. When Luigi saw it, he got up.

"I'll teach you to dig up my garden." She went for him with the broom, but Luigi was too quick for her. He bolted past her, receiving a passing swat on his backside. She chased him around the garden twice. Try as he might, Lowell could not contain his laughter.

Julia stopped in front of Lowell. She had sweat on her brow. "My beautiful rhododendrons. Oh Mr....David. Why, why did he have to dig up my garden?"

Lowell could barely contain his amusement. "Because he's a dog."

"Well, you don't have to enjoy it so much."

He tried to put on a concerned face. "I'm sorry, Julia. We'll get you new bushes, I promise."

"Oh whatever. I'll be glad when he's gone. And that woman, too."

"Yes, me too." He didn't like his routine disrupted. Still, he did enjoy the company of a dog and wondered if he would ever again own one. He couldn't stand to lose them, and every time he had to bury one of his beloved canine friends it broke his heart. That's why he finally decided on turtles. They live a long time.

Julia lifted the broom and resumed her attack. Finally Luigi leaped up the stairs, past the open screen door, and into the house with Julia and her broom only a step behind.

About thirty minutes later Lowell finished the *Times*, picked up his coffee cup, and headed into the house. He walked through the kitchen and into the living room. Julia was asleep on the couch. The broom lay on the floor next to her. Luigi was also asleep on the couch, his head resting in Julia's lap—the picture of total contentment.

Lowell needed to get to his office and learn more about Officer Sweeney and Mickey Broad, and to find out who was after whom.

And if Dr. Williamson was a killer as Karen thought.

Chapter Twenty-three

"Sarah, get me Detective Wally Samuels in L.A. You'll find his number in the files."

"Okay, Boss."

A few moments later his intercom buzzed. He picked up the phone. "Lowell."

"Hey David, nice to hear from you."

"Wally, how's the left coast?"

"Still here. Why? Do the stars say it's time to leave?"

"Not yet. But if we don't change our ways, it shouldn't be long before Arizona is beachfront property." He laughed.

"What can I do for you? I assume this call has to do with our dear Karen Sweeney?"

"Yes," said Lowell. "I'd like to thank you for dropping her in my lap."

"Now David, you've met her. Do you think there's anything I could have done to stop her?"

"Tell me about her."

"She's willful, arrogant, and can be nasty."

"Uh huh. Is she a good cop?"

"One of the best," said Samuels. "She's tenacious and focused, and she can take care of herself."

"That I know." He told Wally about the carjacking incident.

"That's our Karen, always sticking her nose into everything. She's a whiz at martial arts. I think she's overcompensating for her size."

Lowell could hear a lighter flick. "Still smoking, huh?"

"I'm trying to quit. I've tried gum, hypnosis, doctors, everything. Hell, right now I've got my office door locked, and I'm almost hanging out my window. I feel like a criminal every time I light up."

"Good luck with it."

"You ever smoke?"

"Briefly, in my late teens. But I never really liked it and I quit very early on."

"Well, I wish I could. Especially living here in L.A. where everyone's into all this health crap. You should see the looks I get."

"What do you think about all of this?" asked Lowell.

"You mean about Karen being in New York?"

"Yes. Do you think there's something to it?"

He heard Wally take a big puff. "Karen is usually clear-headed and very professional. I know she seems to be a bit of a firecracker, but when it comes to police work she's one hundred percent. But this business is something else. She tell anything about her uncle?"

"Not much."

"I think it's a difficult subject for her. Mickey Broad was more than just her uncle. Karen's father died when she was about ten and in many ways her uncle filled the void. He was close to his sister, Karen's mother, and would often be at their house. He took Karen to ballgames, and sometimes on stakeouts. I think he's the reason she became a cop. She took his death very hard."

"So," said Lowell, "she came east to follow a lead."

Wally puffed again. "And you want to know if this lead is legitimate or if she's just off the deep end."

"Something like that."

Wally cleared his throat. "I can't tell you. Karen has a sixth sense about people. She can sometimes tell right off the bat if someone's lying. But this is so personal I'm just not sure if she's seeing things clearly or not. But I wouldn't reject it out of hand."

"Okay. What do you know about Mickey Broad?"

Samuels took a puff, and then coughed violently. "Damn." He coughed again. "I met him a couple of times through the years, mostly at social functions. He came to a retirement party we had for one of our sergeants and, I think, a Christmas party. But I don't know much about him personally at all. Why?"

"It'll help me understand the situation better if I know who the players are."

"Well, sorry I can't help you there."

"That's alright. I've got my methods."

"What do you think of Luigi?" asked the cop.

"He's redecorating my house for me. Thank God I have Julia or I would be losing my mind."

Samuels laughed. "Well, good luck with it all. And let me know how it works out."

They hung up.

Lowell buzzed Mort. "Get me the birth information for an L.A. detective named Mickey Broad. He was born in New York, sometime in the fifties or early sixties, I would guess, possibly the Lower East Side."

Chapter Twenty-four

Karen showed up at the office at about two that afternoon. Mort was just leaving Lowell's office when she entered.

"Karen Sweeney, this is my associate Mort Simpson. Karen's with the LAPD. She's here to investigate the death of her uncle, the detective from L.A. that I mentioned to you. Apparently Dr. Williamson was one of his last clients, and Karen's trying to establish if he had a role in her uncle's murder."

"Hey, Mort." They shook hands.

"Nice to meet you," said Mort, as he exited.

Karen plopped on the couch, a bottle of Poland Springs water in hand, and looked through her notebook.

"I went out to Queens this morning."

"Did you uncover anything?"

She sipped her water. "My uncle had been to Astoria, I guess that's part of Queens, and I went to the address that I found in his notes. Thanks for having Andy drive me. That's some car you've got."

"Did you find anything useful?"

She shook her head. "A guy named Christo lives there above a deli. I spoke to him briefly. Swears he knows nothing about my uncle. I'd like to tail him later today."

"I hope you do a better job than you did with me."

"Yeah, and I don't think following him in a limo would work too well. I guess I'll take my car out there tomorrow."

"Do you have a GPS in your car?"

"'fraid not."

Lowell tugged on his ponytail. "I have several cars garaged near my home. I think it would be better if you used one of them. They've all got GPS. I'm afraid you may get lost. Andy will drive you up there."

"Thanks."

She picked up the notebook and stood.

"The sooner I get started the better."

Lowell picked up the phone and dialed. "Andy, I'm sending Karen down to you. Please take her to the garage on Ninety-second Street and get the Volvo for her." He was about to hang up. "Oh, and Andy, maybe you should let her follow you back to Astoria. Then she's on her own."

He hung up. "You're all set."

"I'd also like to go to my uncle's apartment later and check his mail again. It's on East Seventh Street and Avenue B. I went there when I first got to New York, but I get lost in this city. I know it's downtown, but where exactly?"

"Alphabet City."

"You're kidding, right? It's really called that?"

"Yep. Avenues A, B, and C in the East Village. I think I'll accompany you when you go, if you don't mind."

"Not at all." She stood and looked at the time on her phone. "Let me see how this goes with the tailing. How about if I call you when I'm done?" She programmed Lowell's cell number into her phone and left.

A few moments later Mort returned.

"What do you think of our guest? Any psychic feelings?"

"Karen?" Mort furrowed his brow. "I think she's just what she appears to be. A hard-nosed cop with an attitude. I think she's a straight-shooter, don't you?"

Lowell nodded. "Yes, I agree. She seems down-to-earth, at least as far as her work goes. And Samuels in L.A. spoke highly of her."

Mort raised his eyebrows. "So you're wondering if she might be onto something with Williamson."

"It's hard to ignore the inconsistencies in his story."

"Let me see what else I can dig up about him." Mort turned to leave.

"Oh, and Mort, see what you can learn about her uncle Mickey Broad."

Mort turned back. "The PI from L.A.? Okay. I already gave you his birth info. Anything else in particular?"

Lowell tugged on his ponytail. "Find out what kind of a detective he was. Was he any good? Did he solve most of his cases? That kind of thing."

Mort nodded. "I'll do a workup on him. Have you looked at his chart?"

"Not yet," admitted the astrologer. "I've been too busy with the embezzlement case. Let me put in his birth information." He turned to his computer screen.

"Okay, Boss. I'll do that workup on the uncle. I'll check in with you later." He left.

Lowell worked for a while but about an hour later started to lose his concentration.

It was eerily silent in the office.

Lowell sat on the couch, lost for a moment in the calm. He knew that the Moon had gone Void of Course a few minutes before, a time of disconnection. Bad for worldly events, but very good for spiritual ones. Lowell wasn't a particularly patient man and preferred action whenever possible. But sometimes you had to wait for the information to come to you.

He got up, buzzed Sarah four times to let her know he wasn't to be disturbed, took off his shoes, sat on the couch, and drew the forefinger to the thumb on each of his hands. Then he closed his eyes and began to meditate. Tranquility engulfed him and his heart rate and pulse slowed to a fraction of their usual speed. He rode the gentle sea of his consciousness atop his mantra, momentarily serene in the oneness of the universe. After about twenty minutes he slowly opened his eyes and allowed his breathing to increase, a little better prepared to deal with the realities of the conscious world.

He got up and walked to the window. He always felt better after a TM session, more relaxed and hopeful. He fed Buster and Keaton and chatted with them for a while.

About an hour later Melinda came in.

"Hi, Dad." She kissed him on his cheek. "I came by to see how things were going, since I'm officially your attorney."

"Good. There are a few things I need to go over with you."

He told her about Karen and Luigi.

"You let a strange woman stay at your townhouse? Dad, that's so unlike you. The dog I can understand, but a person?"

"If you saw the state she was in when I met her you'd understand. They were sleeping in her car parked on the street."

Melinda frowned. "She's lucky she wasn't questioned by the police."

"She's convinced that Williamson had something to do with her uncle's murder and refuses to leave until she finds out the truth."

"So what are you going to do with her?"

"I'm going to help her find her uncle's killer as fast as possible and send her back to L.A."

"Do you think she's right about Williamson?"

"I don't know. But I think you may earn your fee before this is all over." He turned to the computer. "I was just about to look at the charts of Williamson and his wife again."

He printed out a handful of charts, and handed Melinda her own set to peruse.

She looked at them for a few moments. "The comparison is interesting and shows a lot of interaction."

"Yes, but do you see anything unusual about those connections?"

She scrunched her face up. "They're mostly involving connections to the outer planets: Saturn, Uranus, Neptune, and Pluto. Dr. Williamson's Uranus and Pluto are conjunct Gloria's Moon, Sun, and south node. While his Moon and Mercury oppose those planets in her chart. In their composite chart Venus opposes Neptune. These aspects have more to do with how they relate to the collective than the individual."

"Right. What else?"

"The Sun opposes the Moon in the composite chart. That's the only personal aspect I see, and a Full Moon is usually very difficult in a relationship."

Lowell smiled. "Exactly. Usually in a marriage chart it is the inner planets, especially the Sun, Moon, Mercury, Venus, and Mars that are positively connected. That allows the couple to interact successfully on a day-to-day basis. Here the only connection between the personal planets is that Sun-Moon opposition, and it won't help much."

"So wouldn't the lack of constructive and affirmative personal aspects imply that they would have difficulties relating to each other?"

"I would think so. And what Gloria has told me about their marriage certainly makes the point. With outer planet aspects, the marriage would have more of a "fated" sense about it, rather than an easy romantic bond or friendship. Most likely one would try to dominate the other and use the relationship for his or her own personal gain."

Melinda pointed to the charts. "And with Williamson's chart so obviously one of power and manipulation, we can assume he was the one in control."

"That a girl."

Melinda felt like a little girl getting daddy's approval, but smiled despite herself.

"So," said the student, "this wasn't a very pleasant connection, especially for the wife. Perhaps there is a karmic connection through their children."

"Perhaps. Let's see where this path leads."

Chapter Twenty-five

Karen called at five. "I'm heading back into Manhattan." She cursed loudly. "If I can get this damn stupid GPS to work right."

"Where are you?" asked Lowell.

"On something called the Grand Central Parkway. I followed this bozo, Christo out to some town out in Long Island somewhere. Nothing. A neighbor I spoke to recognized him. He was visiting his sister."

"Are you heading east or west?"

"West."

"It's simple. Turn the GPS off." He gave her directions. "When you get to the toll on the Tri-Borough Bridge go through the automatic lane. The car has an E-Z-Pass on the windshield that will allow you through. I'll have Andy meet you at the garage and then pick me up and we'll head downtown to your uncle's place."

Andy drove Lowell and Karen to her late uncle's apartment on Avenue B. Julia had to go food shopping and wouldn't let Luigi stay in the house unsupervised, so they took him with them.

Alphabet City is officially part of the East Village, but has its own flavor, and so far had been spared the modernization that most of Manhattan was going through. It's very similar to what the Village had been like many years ago. It still had an old world look and feel about it. Dozens of small shops and restaurants dotted the area. Darkly lit bars offered cheap, by

Manhattan standards, food and drinks, many with live music. The neighborhood surrounded Tompkins Square Park and had a bohemian feeling that reminded Lowell of the Sixties.

As they headed for the apartment they passed a number of residents on stoops and in outdoor cafes. Many of the men had long hair, a rarity uptown. Lowell was suddenly very aware of his ponytail.

They walked up the three steps to the entrance of the building, a small but relatively new structure for this area, probably built in the sixties. The front door was propped open and two men were carrying a dresser out. Lowell and Karen let them pass and then entered.

Karen walked over to the mailbox. "I came here when I first got to town hoping the package he sent had arrived. Boy, talk about snail mail."

She took out the smaller key her uncle had given her and opened the mailbox. Inside was a tiny package, about the size of a cassette tape.

"Well," she said, "it's about time."

She took it out and put it in her pocket. Then they climbed the stairs to the third floor where she took out the other key and opened the door. It was a one room flat about three hundred square feet. Against one wall were a small dresser and a single bed. There was a kitchen table, with two small metal chairs in the middle of the room next to the wall-unit kitchen, and a small loveseat against the opposite wall, all well-worn furniture. In the corner was a small desk with a single drawer. An old lamp sat on top. There wasn't much, but still the room felt cluttered.

Luigi was busy sniffing around the place. Lowell sat on the loveseat. "Let's see what's in that package."

Karen sat next to him, opened the small parcel and tipped it. A tiny plastic envelope surrounded by bubble wrap tumbled out and landed on the table. She picked it up and took the bubble wrap off. Inside the envelope was a computer thumb drive.

Karen handed Lowell the tiny device, about two inches in length.

Lowell turned it over a few times. "Let's get this back to my office and see what's on it."

He got up from the couch and glanced out the window. He saw the same two men who had accosted him and Sarah exiting a car. He watched as they entered the building.

"Karen, do you have your gun with you?"

"No, I left it at your house. Why?"

"We're about to have visitors." He picked up his cell phone and quickly sent a short text. Then he looked around the tiny apartment. "We have to hide this. But where?" The room was so tiny and sparsely furnished it wouldn't take long to search it. There was little time. He walked over to the miniscule kitchen and opened the refrigerator. Inside was an open yogurt, a bottle of water, and a new, sealed package of Swiss cheese. He thought about putting the device in the ice tray, but they would find it.

There was a roll of scotch tape on the kitchen counter. He took the thumb drive and taped it to underside of Luigi's collar. Then he pointed across the room to the airshaft at the back of the building. "Throw the packaging out that window."

Karen hurried across the room, opened the window, and threw out the box.

Moments later the door burst open and the two men barged their way in. The one with the long scar on the side of his face, McFarley, according to Lieutenant Roland, held a gun and aimed it at Luigi.

"Alright, get over there and sit down or I'll shoot the dog."

Lowell and Karen sat on the couch.

"What do you want?" asked Lowell.

McFarley walked over toward the couch. Luigi nudged him with his head. The man unconsciously started scratching the dog's ear. His hand nearly brushed against the thumb drive several times as Lowell watched, unable to act.

McFarley pointed at Lowell. "Someone wants you out of the way."

"Who?" asked the detective.

The man shrugged. "It's just a job. Someone wants you gone and I got paid. That's all I care about. Hey, don't take it personally." Then he laughed a boisterous guffaw and waved the gun. "Get up. We're going for a ride."

"Listen, McFarley," said Lowell. "I can pay you much more than they are."

The gunman looked puzzled. "So, you know who I am?"

Lowell nodded.

"Well, that's just too bad for you."

"We can make a deal," said Lowell.

"Shut up," said McFarley. "Stand up. Now."

Lowell tried to reason with him. "You're making a big mistake."

"Yeah, probably ain't the first time." He turned to his partner. "Don't you love how they beg and bargain when they know it's their time? Don't ya just love it?" He laughed again. "Now get up."

There was a pounding on the door.

"Open the door, it's the super."

"McFarley aimed the gun at Lowell. "Get rid of him."

"Okay, just don't do anything stupid." Lowell went to the door and opened it a crack. "What's the problem?"

"I need to get in there. There's been a report of a gas leak and I've called Con Edison. There should be someone here in a few minutes."

The gunman had his weapon in Lowell's back. "Just give me a minute. My wife's dressing."

"Okay, but make it quick. This is serious business."

Lowell went to close the door, but suddenly moved aside. The door was slammed open and hit McFarley in the face, knocking him backwards. Andy rushed in, his own gun drawn.

The other man was standing next to the loveseat. He took a gun out of his pocket and aimed it at Andy. Karen jumped up from the sofa and shoved herself against the man just as the gun went off. The shot missed Andy by inches. The gunman was getting ready to fire again. Andy turned and with a calm look in his eye, aimed his gun and fired, hitting the man in the chest, killing him instantly.

McFarley ran past Andy knocking the gun out of his hand. He ran out the door and down the stairs before anyone could react.

Andy picked up his gun. "You want me to chase him?"

Lowell shook his head. "Let him go. They were just hired hands. I don't think there's much we can learn from him anyway. Let the police deal with him. Karen, you've met Andy."

She waved. "How wonderful to see you again. Your timing couldn't have been better."

"Thank God for texts. Glad I could help." Andy looked down at the body and then turned to Lowell. "Okay, Boss, now what?"

Lowell dialed Melinda. "Andy just killed a man in self-defense. Can you call Lieutenant Roland and meet us here as soon as you're free?" He gave her the address and hung up.

Andy looked shaken up. He sat on the edge of the tiny bed. "You know I was in the Corps." Lowell nodded. "I killed people before. But this is different. Most of them were a long ways off, not in your face."

Lowell had been responsible for the death of a man in the Judge Winston case and knew the feelings it could create. There was a sense of karma—that this act would never completely leave you and would even follow you into future lifetimes. Lowell was a firm believer in reincarnation.

Andy continued. "I know it's part of the job, and hell, he was a piece of dirt who was gonna kill us if he could. It's just that, I don't know, sometimes I wish I did something else for a living. You know?"

Lowell knew.

"Andy, if you ever get the itch to try something else, no matter how off the track it may seem, please come to me and I'm sure we can work it out."

Andy nodded. Then he smiled. "Well, for now I'm still your bodyguard and chauffeur."

"And friend."

Chapter Twenty-six

About twenty minutes later Roland arrived with two uniforms. Melinda was just a few moments behind. Roland nodded to her as she entered. "How are you, Melinda. Haven't seen you in a while. You're looking well."

"Hi Phil, how have you been?"

Roland shook his head. "Tough business."

Melinda walked over to Karen. "I'm Melinda Lowell, David's daughter." She stuck out her hand.

Karen shook it forcefully. "Karen Sweeney. How nice to meet you."

The lieutenant walked over to Lowell. "What happened?"

Lowell tugged at his ponytail. "Lieutenant Philip Roland, Officer Karen Sweeney of the Los Angeles Police Department. This is her uncle's apartment."

Roland ran his fingers through his hair. He sighed. "Why do I think this isn't going to make me happy?" He turned to Karen. "What can I do for the LAPD?"

"Well…" she started.

Lowell interrupted. "Actually, Karen isn't working officially for the department at the moment. She's here on personal business."

"I see," said Roland. "May I ask what personal business?"

"I'm here to find my uncle's murderer."

"And your uncle was…?"

"Mickey Broad," said Karen, "a private eye from L.A."

"This was his place?"

Karen nodded.

"And he was killed in N.Y.?" asked Roland.

She shook her head. "No, L.A."

The cop frowned. "Then why am I so lucky to have you in my jurisdiction?"

"He was in New York shortly before his death and I'm here following a lead."

Roland nodded. "Just stay within the law and I've got no problem with that. Are you carrying?"

"I have my piece at David's place."

Roland cast a glance at Lowell, his mouth turning up just at the very corners. "At David's place?" Luigi walked over to Roland and pushed his head up into the lieutenant's hand. Roland unconsciously scratched Luigi's head. "Your dog?"

Karen nodded. "That's Luigi."

Roland smiled and turned toward Lowell. "He staying at your place too?"

Lowell nodded, a slight grimace on his face.

The cop grinned broadly. "So what happened here?"

"Karen wanted to see her uncle's place and look around a bit," said Lowell. "We were getting ready to leave when the deceased and McFarley pushed their way in."

"McFarley again?" asked Roland.

Lowell nodded. "Right before they broke in I texted Andy and let him know what was happening." Lowell pointed to the wall and then to the dead man. "You'll find a bullet over there that came from this guy's gun. Andy only shot in self-defense."

Roland spoke to one of the uniformed policemen. "Dig that slug out of the wall and bag it." He turned to Lowell. "The forensic team will be here soon and they can go over it all."

"Do you need us here?" asked Lowell.

Roland shook his head. "I'm going to have to take your driver to the precinct, but it's only a formality." He turned to Andy. "Frankly, I wish you had gotten that other piece of garbage."

Andy nodded. "No time, or I would have."

Roland took out a cellphone and dialed. "It's Roland. McFarley was involved in a possible hit gone bad. I don't care what it takes, I want that SOB in custody now. Find him. Circulate his picture to everyone." He hung up,

Melinda walked over. "Lieutenant, do you think Andy needs a lawyer?"

Roland shook his head. "I don't think so. It looks like a righteous shooting. Is your permit in order?"

Andy nodded and opened his wallet. "Here's my license to carry."

Roland looked at it and returned it to Andy. He turned to Melinda. "If there are any legal problems I'll let you know."

"Thank you, Phil," she said.

Lowell was getting antsy. "Can we leave?"

Roland turned to Lowell and Karen. "I'm gonna need statements from you two. Might as well get it over with now."

He called over one of the officers. "Wilson, take down their statements."

"Okay, Lieutenant," said the officer.

"And Wilson," said Roland, "try to make it legible, will ya?"

The officer smiled and took out a small digital recorder. "Got it covered," he said. "They can type it up at the precinct."

When they finished telling their tale, Lowell, Melinda, and Karen left. Lowell was forced to drive the limo home. Although he enjoyed driving on certain occasions, and would at times take a journey by himself out of New York, navigating that huge car in the city wasn't much fun. He managed to get them home without incident.

Chapter Twenty-seven

As they entered the townhouse Julia greeted them at the door. When Luigi saw Julia he lunged toward her and leaped up onto his back legs putting his front paws on her shoulders and lapping her face.

She tolerated the licking for a few moments. "Okay, that's enough. Get down." A stern look on her face. He went on all fours and then sat, looking up at her with anticipation. She took out a kitchen cloth from her apron pocket and wiped her face. "I suppose you want to eat again?"

He cocked his head to the side and stared at her.

"Supper?"

He got up, tail wagging fervently and pranced into the kitchen a step ahead of Julia who turned back halfway down the hall. "I swear he understands English better than I do."

The others walked into the living room. Lowell sat in the armchair. Karen and Melinda sat on the couch.

Melinda looked at her father. "Did you find anything at the apartment?"

"There was a tiny thumb drive in the mail."

"Why aren't we downstairs in your office looking through it?"

"Well, we don't actually have it at the moment. I had to hide it."

Melinda saw her father smirk. "So who has it?"

Just then Luigi came bounding into the room, as if on cue, licking the remnants of his supper from his lips. He sat at Karen's feet. Lowell pointed to him.

"He does."

Melinda and Luigi both cocked their heads to the right at the same time. "Really? And when do you think he'll give it back?"

Lowell clapped his hands and Luigi came over. He took hold of the dog's collar and pealed off the taped thumb drive. "Here it is."

"Well?" said Melinda. "Let's go see what's on this device that's so important."

They went down to the townhouse basement office. Luigi chose to stay close to Julia. You never knew when an errant morsel might find its way onto the floor. Lowell turned on the computer and popped the thumb drive into the USB port and tried to open the files.

"There's a password." He turned to Karen. "Any ideas?"

"None at the moment. I'd have to think about it."

Lowell dialed Mort and put him on speakerphone.

"What's up, Boss?"

"Sorry to bother you, but we've got a thumb drive from Karen's uncle and we need to get the password."

Mort's voice filled the room. "Karen, did you talk to your uncle often?"

"Yeah, all the time."

Mort was silent for a moment. Lowell could imagine him at home furrowing his brow as he often did while trying to use his psychic intuition. "I think it's something you know very well. Did you discuss a password for anything?"

Karen frowned. "Not that I remember."

The speakerphone was silent for a few moments. The Mort's voice returned.

"It's something you've discussed with him many times. He wanted to make sure you could work it out, if necessary. Did you two have a favorite sports team, or nickname?"

"Not really."

Mort suddenly laughed.

"You know what it is, don't you?" asked Lowell.

"Yes, I think so. It's…"

"Luigi." Lowell and Mort said at the same time.

Mort's booming laugh filled the room. "Try it."

Lowell typed in the dog's name and the files popped open. "It worked."

"Hey, you two are good," said Karen. "See, everyone loves Luigi."

"Thanks Mort, I'll see you in the morning." Lowell hung up. Then he scrolled through the files and printed copies of a dozen items. He looked through each quickly as they popped into the tray, and then handed them to Melinda. "Well, you're my legal expert. What do you think?"

She took the pages and read through them. When she was done she put them on the desk, stood up and stretched. "Karen, I think there may be something to your theory."

"Why? What's it say?"

"It says that Dr. Edgar Williamson might very well be a crook."

Lowell spoke. "There's a record of several genetic patents Williamson owned and how he acquired them, including the one involving Francis Goldsmith, a woman who was suing Williamson when she died in a hit and run. Apparently Mrs. Goldsmith was just about to get her case into court when she had her most unfortunate accident. Quite a coincidence."

"And my father doesn't believe in coincidences."

"No, I don't. There's also a note here about a cash layout of fifty thousand dollars to something called A-One Security Services at the same time." He made a mental note to have Mort follow up on the name.

Karen started to pace. "So what does all this mean?"

Lowell leaned back in his chair. "Williamson owns a number of valuable patents. How he acquired the blood samples used to extract that DNA has everything to do with legal ownership. If they were obtained from discarded blood, it's considered public property. If they were taken directly from the patient for the purposes of research, they are that patient's property. Of course, all of this may become moot as a result of the Supreme Court's recent ruling that nobody can own an exclusive patent on DNA and how that is interpreted.

He handed Karen the paper. "That's a sworn statement from the attending nurse who was present at the time of Mrs. Goldsmith's examination. According to this, Williamson did his research on blood that he took directly from Mrs. Goldsmith's body for the sole purpose of experimenting and patenting it, not from discarded samples, as he claimed, which would make the acquisition illegal. Your uncle may have been on the verge of proving that Williamson did not, in fact, own the patent."

"What's it worth?" asked Karen.

Lowell slipped off his loafers and put his feet up on the edge of the desk. "Likely millions. I wonder where your uncle got this." He leaned back in his chair. "Melinda, what do you think?"

"Well, it may show that he was a crook, but there's nothing here to prove murder."

"I agree."

Karen wasn't sold. "If ten years with the LAPD has taught me anything, it's that one thread leads to another. Uncle Mickey found out that Williamson stole this woman's DNA, and he was dead soon after. I find that a coincidence I can't accept."

"Okay," said Lowell, "maybe you're right. But even if Williamson had stolen it, why would he risk murdering your uncle for something so difficult to prove? Mrs. Goldsmith is long dead and the DA would be loath to reexamine her accident now based solely on this nurse's testimony." He tugged on his ponytail and sighed deeply. "I don't think this is why your uncle was killed."

Karen stopped pacing. "What about those two thugs? They must have been after those files."

"We don't even know who hired McFarley," said Lowell. "I'm working on several cases at the moment. He didn't mention the thumb drive once. I don't think he was even aware of its existence. They may have just followed us to your uncle's place. I think there's something else amiss here. Something that we're missing. I'll let Mort examine the files tomorrow."

Lowell got up, closed the computer, and headed toward the stairs. "In the meantime, I don't know the answer. But I'll be better able to look at it with a fresh perspective in the morning. Good night, ladies."

Chapter Twenty-eight

"Mort, here's the thumb drive Karen's uncle sent. I want you to go through it and see if there's anything I missed. Track down a company called A-One Security Services that Mickey Broad referred to. There's also someone named Maria Rodriguez mentioned several times. See if you can find out who she is."

Lowell handed Mort the tiny device. "Have you found out anything else about the uncle?"

Mort was sitting in a client's chair. "He ran a one-man operation out of L.A. Usually he took one case at a time. He didn't put much on the Internet and there's no way for me to tell what he was working on, unless I go out to California and look through his files."

"I don't think that's necessary."

Mort smiled. "That's too bad. I could use a few days by the beach."

Lowell chuckled. "Maybe next time."

Mort flapped his arms. "I'll start on this now."

He took the thumb drive and headed for his office.

About an hour later Mort entered Lowell's office waving a piece of paper.

Lowell looked up. "So what have you got for me?"

"A-One Securities is a small operation out of Jersey City. From what I can gather they operate just barely within the law.

Seems to be mostly strong-arm tactics specializing in intimidation and harassment."

Lowell took this in and jotted down a few lines. "What about the woman?"

"Maria Rodriguez. She lives on the other side of Clifton about three miles from the hospital."

"What have you got on her?"

"Ms. Rodriguez has a degree in anesthesiology from a small medical college in upstate New York. She's worked at Williamson's hospital for the past three years."

"Okay, so she knows Williamson. Any connection beyond that?"

"I've got a few pictures of them together at a charity ball the hospital threw about a year ago. But there isn't much more. But I'll do a more thorough background on her."

"Soon, please. Get me anything about her that seems pertinent."

Mort got a strange glint in his eye. "Say, I have an idea. Do you know where Karen is?"

"I think she's at the townhouse. Why?"

"I think I'll do a little detective work."

Lowell raised his eyebrows.

Karen and Mort sat in Lowell's Volvo. Karen was behind the wheel. Although he had a license, Mort wasn't fond of driving and rarely did so.

"That's her house," said Mort, as he took a sip of coffee.

It was a small, simple abode with a picket fence in front of a diminutive lawn. A large oak took up much of the front yard, its branches producing a welcome summertime shade. On one side of the tree sat a swing set, long abandoned. One swing was broken, hanging on by a single chain. Rust lined the poles. A red Ford sat parked in the driveway.

"So now what?"

"Now," said the cop, "we wait. Haven't you ever been on a stakeout before?"

Mort shook his head. "David doesn't usually work like this."

"Well, I don't know how you guys manage."

Mort took a swig of Poland Springs water. "Mostly we work from the office using astrology and the Internet. Although we do occasionally break a few laws." He laughed, then reached into the backseat and grabbed a bag from a deli. "I'm just glad you had me pick up sandwiches. You want one?"

He took out a chicken salad on rye and started eating.

She shook her head. "I'll wait a little while. You never know how long you may have to sit."

They were silent for a few minutes.

Mort looked over at her, his mouth loaded with chicken salad. He scrunched up his face. "He's coming back."

Karen turned to him. "What? Why would you say that?"

"Well, that is what you were thinking about, isn't it? Your boyfriend left angry and you're afraid it's over. Don't worry, when you get back to L.A. there'll be a message. He wants to come back and try again. Bob, or Bruce, something like that."

"Burt." She half-closed her eyes and looked at him. "You're a little funky, you know that?"

Mort laughed uproariously and slapped his knee.

"Could you always do that?"

"Ever since I was a kid. I always knew when the phone was about to ring and often who was calling. And I could just tell things about people when I'd sit next to them."

Karen shook her head. "Damnedest thing I ever saw."

They were silent again.

"Also, you should have that shoulder looked at. It's getting worse."

Karen just shook her head and laughed.

About an hour later the front door opened and an attractive dark-haired woman, wearing a red dress just about the color of the car, exited. She got into the red Ford and backed out of the driveway. Karen waited until she was about half a block ahead and then began to follow.

They drove on a two-lane road into Clifton and out the other side. The Ford made a right onto a country highway and out into the Jersey suburbs. They passed through several small towns and finally the car pulled into an out-of-the-way motel. Karen parked off to the side and they watched.

Maria got out of the car and went into the office. She came out a few moments later with a key in her hand. Then she took out her iPhone, sent a text, and went into cabin number three.

Mort was anxious. "Now what?"

Their wait was quite short. A few minutes later a blue Jaguar pulled up only a few spaces from where they sat. The door opened and Dr. Williamson stepped from the car. He walked over to cabin number three, opened the door, and entered, closing the door behind him.

"Well," said Mort, "will you look at that?"

Karen grinned. "Yep. Okay, so the doctor and the anesthesiologist are involved. So what? What could be so important about Ms. Rodriguez that my uncle would put her name into the files? Surely not just because they're having an affair."

Mort took out his cellphone. "That's what we're going to find out. Let's head back to the office."

◇◇◇

"So Williamson is involved with Maria Rodriguez. That's very interesting." Lowell sat back in his chair. "Mort, have you gotten anything else on them?"

"Not really. Just those party pictures."

"Well, keep digging."

Karen was excited. "There's got to be a reason my uncle included her in those files. At least this is a clue."

Lowell nodded. "We will certainly follow up on Maria Rodriguez."

"I'd like to keep tailing her."

Lowell tried to be diplomatic. "It takes at least three people to successfully tail someone covertly."

She nodded. "I know. I just can't sit here on my hands, and there's nothing else I can do."

"Why don't you and Mort see what you can dig up on Ms. Rodriguez and if you find a lead I'll be happy to follow up?"

Chapter Twenty-nine

When Lowell arrived at the office at seven-thirty, he found an overnight package from the post office waiting outside the door. The return address had a picture of a dancing marshmallow complete with top hat and cane. He wondered how they managed to get away with copying the Mr. Peanut logo so closely. He opened the office door and entered, turned on Sarah's lamp, and left the package on her desk. Then he entered his inner office, fed Buster and Keaton, and got to work.

At nine exactly Sarah buzzed twice. Lowell returned her buzz.

A few moments later she knocked and opened the door. "Hey boss," she said, as she stuffed a red marshmallow into her mouth. "God, these things are delicious. I think this one is strawberry, or maybe raspberry. Want one?"

Lowell shook his head. He used to love the sweet gelatin-based treats, ever since childhood, but had to give them up once he stopped eating meat. He wondered if Buddy made a vegan product. "No thanks. What've you got for me?"

She swallowed the gooey delight. "You don't know what you're missing. Although they are messy." She was trying to clean her teeth with her tongue. "You've got twenty-seven messages. It'll take me a while to get through them all."

"We've got a busy day ahead. Mark down any that are directly connected to the two active cases and leave the rest for later."

She went back to her desk. Lowell worked on the charts of the bookkeeper, Harriet, and her brother. He was trying to decide what the best course of action would be. Both charts showed the possibility of incarceration, but nothing was guaranteed.

At nine-thirty Mort entered. He was nibbling on a green marshmallow.

"It's lime-flavored," he said, as he popped the rest of it into his mouth.

Lowell grimaced. "I'm waiting to see what the Feds say about the embezzlement case. Not much more we can do right now."

Mort flapped his arms. "How about Williamson?"

"I'm also on hold there waiting to hear from him about the operation."

Mort watched his friend's face. "This case is bothering you, isn't it?"

Lowell nodded. "Yes, something's just not right about all of this. I'll know better once I hear from him. For now, I need you to do some digging into the background of the bookkeeper and her brother."

"Anything in particular?"

"I want to know if they have property outside the U.S. Also what their general financial situation is. Do they have any money? Any prior arrests or maybe IRS troubles?"

Mort's head bobbed up and down. "Okay, I'll get right on it." He went back to his office.

◇◇◇

About eleven Lowell's intercom buzzed.

"Yes Sarah?'

"Buddy Ferguson is on line two."

"Lowell."

"Mr. Lowell, I've just heard from the FBI."

"Buddy, are your phones any more secured than they were?"

"Well, I've got my door closed, but I suppose someone could be listening."

Lowell rubbed his eyes while shaking his head. "I'd better come over."

"I'm here all day."

Lowell hung up and then dialed Melinda.

"Hi, Dad, what's up?"

"I have to go to the marshmallow company, and I was wondering if you were free later to compare notes."

"I'm busy all day, but I can meet you at the townhouse after work."

"Okay," he said. "I'll call you later."

Lowell hung up, left the office, and met Andy in front of the building.

◇◇◇

Twenty minutes later he entered the marshmallow company and was quickly ushered into Buddy's office. Buddy closed the door behind them.

"So what did the FBI come up with?"

Buddy opened the plastic container and began eating. "Agent Bill Jensen is in charge. He's reluctant to examine the bank's records and said you have to have more evidence before he'll order it."

"I'll talk to him," said Lowell.

"I wish you would. Maybe you can convince him of the severity of the situation. People who have worked for us, some for more than twenty years, are in danger of losing their retirement accounts. That's got to be important enough for them to investigate, don't you think?"

"Yes, I would think so. Give me his number."

Buddy wrote the number on a piece of paper and handed it to Lowell. "You still think it's Harriet and her brother?"

"I do. Of the birth dates you gave me, her chart was the most likely. But once I saw her brother's that clinched it. Now we need the proof that only the FBI can obtain."

"Well, Harriet often works from home, but she's working here today if you'd like to see her."

Lowell thought about it. "That might be a good idea."

"Just take a walk to the left toward the bathroom at the end of the hall. Her office is the last one on the right."

Lowell got up and headed down the hall. He went toward the men's room, but as he passed by he glanced into the bookkeeper's office. The door was open and behind the desk sat a woman about forty, with longish blond hair pulled back into a bun. She wore a green dress and black flats, little make up, and no jewelry, except for a single ring on her left hand. She was focused on her paperwork, her concentration on the task at hand. As Lowell passed by she looked up. Their eyes met briefly, and then she put her head back down. The glance was fleeting, but it said volumes to Lowell. There was something wrong in that look.

He went into the bathroom to complete the subterfuge, washed his hands, and returned to Buddy's office.

"Well," asked Buddy, "what'd you think?"

Lowell sat. "What I've thought all along. She did it."

Buddy's smile almost faded from his rotund face. "Harriet, of all people. But will you be able to prove it?"

"I hope so. I'll let you know what happens after I speak to Agent Jensen."

Buddy nodded, and then grabbed an almost fluorescent looking yellow goodie. Lowell stared at it, a slightly sickened look on his face.

"It's banana cream pie, a new flavor we're trying out. Would you like one?" He ate it.

Lowell shook his head. "Thanks, but I'll pass."

"Did you get the box I sent over to your office?"

"Yes, I did. Thank you. My staff is enjoying them immensely, especially Sarah."

Buddy's smile widened. "My pleasure. Just let me know if you need any more." He shuffled some papers half-heartedly and then threw them down on his desk. "I just can't concentrate until this is settled. It's just really so depressing." His smile faded momentarily.

Lowell got up to leave. "I understand. I'll call Agent Jensen today and see what he has to say. I'll let you know as soon as I have any more information."

Chapter Thirty

Lowell left the building and headed uptown to his office. It was a beautiful day for walking, not too hot or humid, with an almost-autumn like breeze coming from the East River. He texted Andy and gave him his route, then he started up First Avenue.

At Sixteenth Street the light was with him and he started to cross. His phone rang and he stopped to take it out of his pocket. He stepped back onto the sidewalk just as a light colored SUV darted out from the traffic on First Avenue and made a sharp right hand turn down Sixteenth, missing Lowell by barely an inch. Had he not stopped he would surely have been killed. The SUV continued speeding down the street. He was shaken up. He answered the phone but had to catch his breath before speaking.

"Hello? Dad?"

Melinda's voice was enough to smack him back to reality. "Hello?"

"Dad, are you alright?"

"I was almost killed just now in an accident crossing the street."

"Are you sure it was an accident?"

"I'm not sure of anything."

"Where are you?"

"Walking up First. I just left the marshmallow company."

"Get into a cab."

"Andy'll be here in a few minutes. I'll be fine."

"Call me when you're at the office, okay?"

"Melinda, I'm fine, really. I'm sure it was just someone from New Jersey. You know how they drive in the city."

She was not amused.

"Here's Andy now. I'll call you later."

He hung up. Andy pulled the limo to the sidewalk and Lowell got in.

"What's up boss?"

Lowell told Andy what had happened.

"You want to go to the office?"

Lowell shook his head. "I want to look for that SUV. Maybe they haven't gotten out of the neighborhood yet."

"Sure, I'll cruise around a little. What color was it?"

"Tan. And I think it was a Chevy."

Andy went down Eighteenth Street and turned north on First Avenue. No sign of the SUV. They rode around the East Side for about twenty minutes when Lowell spotted it on Twelfth Street.

"Andy, there it is, up ahead at the light."

Andy floored the limo and had almost caught up to the SUV when a car jolted out of a parking space and almost ran into them. The wheels of the limo squealed their displeasure as Andy slammed on the brakes just missing the car. He pulled around it just as the SUV went through the light.

"Were you able to see the license plate?" asked Lowell.

"Sorry boss, couldn't get it."

They waited for the light to change and hurried through the intersection heading west in the direction the SUV had taken. At Ninth Avenue, Andy spotted it again.

"They're heading downtown."

"Follow them," said Lowell.

They were only a few cars behind when a city bus pulled out in front of the limo and stopped. "Boss, there's no way around him."

When the bus finally moved on, there was no sight of the SUV.

After another thirty minutes they gave up. Andy swung back east and dropped Lowell at the office.

When he came in Sarah was waiting anxiously for him. "What happened? Melinda called and said you were almost run over."

"Sarah, it was an accident. Let's not make more out of it than it deserves."

He went into his office and called his daughter. "I'm at the office."

"What do you think is going on?"

"I'm sure it was just an acc…"

"Dad!"

He sighed. "Alright. I don't know what's going on. I've got those cases that are very active at the moment."

"Any others on the back burner that someone might be trying to scare you off of or kill you before you even get started?"

"I don't know."

"This is not making me happy."

"Try not to worry," said Lowell. "I'll be fine."

He hung up and almost immediately the intercom buzzed. "Yes Sarah?"

"It's Buddy on line one."

Lowell picked up the phone. "Yes, Buddy?"

"Harriet's gone. Right after you left, she got up and just walked out without saying a word. She's never done that in the fifteen years I've know her. What does it mean?"

"It means that we've got to move quickly or you'll never get your pension fund back."

"Oh hell," said Buddy.

"Buddy, do you know what type of car Harriet drives?"

"Not off hand. Is it important?"

"I was almost run over after leaving your office this morning."

Buddy gasped. "Surely you don't think Harriet had anything to do with it, do you?"

"I don't believe in coincidences. The fact that it happened moments after she and I saw each other for the first time makes me rather suspicious. It may have been a random accident, or it could have been her or her brother."

"Oh," said Buddy, "this is all just too much for me." Lowell could hear him chewing. "Please let me know anything that you discover."

Lowell hung up and buzzed Mort.

"What's up, David?"

"I want you to find out if the bookkeeper or her brother owns a tan SUV, maybe a Chevy." He gave Mort the brother's name and the bank he worked for. "And find out his birth information."

"Will do."

Lowell buzzed Sarah. "Get me FBI headquarters." He gave her the number. "I want to speak to Agent Jensen."

Chapter Thirty-one

The FBI New York headquarters was located at 26 Federal Plaza on lower Broadway. The offices were on the twenty-third floor and looked the way one would expect. Simple, sterile, spartan. They made Lowell's office look ornate by comparison. Lowell was ushered into Agent Jensen's office where he was met by two men.

One was about six feet tall with brown hair just starting to gray around the temples. He stood up and stuck out his hand. "Mr. Lowell, I'm Special Agent Jensen and this is Special Agent Anderson."

The other man rose. They shook hands.

"Now," continued Jensen, "what is this all about?"

"Are you familiar with my work?" asked the astrologer.

Jensen nodded. "Buddy Ferguson told me you were involved in this embezzlement and I did a little homework. You were quite impressive on a few cases. But…" He stopped and turned his hands up.

"You have your doubts about my abilities."

The agent looked a little uncomfortable. "You must understand…"

Lowell held up his hand. "I understand completely. You wouldn't be the first person to question the validity of astrology."

The agent seemed relieved.

Lowell took out his laptop. "Would you be willing to give me your birth information? Or perhaps that of someone close to you?"

The agent smirked. "Knock yourself out." He thought for a moment. "You could've looked me up already and found out things about my life."

"True," admitted the astrologer. "So give me someone else's."

Jensen thought for a moment. "Do you have to know who it is?"

Lowell tugged on his ponytail. "Not at all."

"Okay. July 10th, 1968."

"I don't suppose there's any chance you know the time of birth and the city?"

"As a matter of fact, I do. It's 11:12 in the morning in Boston."

Lowell began entering the information into his computer. Then he put the chart up on the screen along with the current transits. "Well, this is quite an active chart. This person is quite nervous and easily upset. He or she is fidgety and accident prone. The planet Uranus sits on the ascendant and is in square to Mercury. Car accidents are very possible. Also their health, in particular the lungs and bronchial tubes are susceptible to difficulties or sudden events. Asthma or other breathing disorders are common.

"This is a Full Moon baby with the Sun in Cancer conjunct Venus in opposition to the Moon in Capricorn. This person is quite charming, possibly very beautiful. But with both the Full Moon and Mars so close to the Sun there could be a bad temper. Emotional issues get blown out of proportion at times. This person's parents had a difficult relationship and probably divorced. He or she inherited a lot of emotional baggage from that separation and has been struggling with it all since childhood. Because the Moon is in the 4th house they probably lived with the mother through childhood. By the way, therapy would be a good idea.

"Saturn is in square to Venus. There is shyness behind the boisterous outer appearance and bouts of sadness that can make this person withdraw into themselves. There is a limitation to the amount of fun this person allows. Also there is a tendency toward difficulty with the kidneys, especially kidney stones."

He punched in another set of charts.

"The Solar Arc Directed chart showed that the divorce probably happened about age four as Uranus was crossing the ascendant. Also Pluto crossed the ascendant when she was nine, and there may have been a violent event, possibly motivated by vengeance or a power struggle, that ended badly."

He looked up at the agent. "There is much more, of course, but that's what I can see in these few minutes. Would you like to hear more?"

Agent Jensen opened his mouth, and then closed it. Then he said, "What can I do for you Mr. Lowell?"

"I have a strong reason to believe that Harriet Collins with the help of her brother John embezzled the retirement fund from the marshmallow company. And I think time is of the essence. If you don't move quickly the money will be transferred off-shore and the two of them will disappear forever."

Jensen was pensive for a few moments, and then he picked up the phone. "Bill, get that court order for the bank…Yes, I believe them."

He hung up. "It'll be done this afternoon."

Agent Andersen grabbed Jensen's arm. "Are you sure about this?"

Jensen turned to his colleague. "That was my wife's birth information, and virtually everything this man said about her is accurate."

Andersen looked over at Lowell, a scowl on his face. "It could be a scam. Maybe he found all of this on the Internet."

"My wife is a very nervous, overly emotional woman," said Jensen. "When she was four, her parents divorced. About five year later the house she shared with her mother was burned to the ground by her father who kidnapped her. He spent ten years in prison, and she spent fifteen years in therapy. She's survived several car crashes. She also suffers from chronic bronchitis, and has had kidney stones twice. I don't think all that information is on the Internet."

Jensen turned to Lowell looking a bit pale, thought the astrologer. He took a sip of water. "I'll let you know what we uncover at the bank."

Lowell got up to leave. "Let's hope we're not too late."

Chapter Thirty-two

Lowell left the FBI headquarters and entered the limo. This was no time to take a stroll uptown unguarded. He looked at his watch. It was almost five o'clock. There wasn't much he could do with this case until he heard from Jensen.

"Andy, I want to pick up Melinda. Let me call her and see where she is."

He dialed.

"Hi Dad."

"I'm heading uptown," said Lowell. "Are you free for dinner? I need to go over a few things with you."

"I'm in my office. I couldn't get out of here before six. Why don't I meet you at the townhouse?"

"I just won't feel right until this embezzlement thing is behind us." He retied his ponytail. "I think I'll just drive around for a while and we'll pick you up in an hour. How's that?"

"Okay, Dad. If it makes you feel better."

"It will. I won't relax until they've caught McFarley."

Lowell hung up. "Andy, you heard?"

"You wanna take a drive until we get Melinda. Gotcha, Boss." Andy pushed a button on the steering wheel and the glass opaque partition between the front seat and the rest of the limo came up. Lowell looked out the window at Manhattan at rush hour, crowded, overwhelming. He shook his head and twisted the knobs on his console. The windows darkened and suddenly the coast of Southern California appeared to be zipping by. He enjoyed the illusion, and why not? It was better than a movie. You were more involved. Your life went on within the car but the world outside was changed. He opened the little refrigerator and took out a Spatan beer and a chilled mug. He poured the beer and sat back enjoying the passing view. When the limo appeared to pass Vivian Younger's house, he tipped his beer in a toast.

They picked up Melinda at six. She came down the steps from her office building and approached the car. "Hi Andy." She gave him a peck on the cheek as Andy held the door for her. She got into the limo and kissed her dad.

"How was your day?" asked Lowell.

"Oh, you know, just the usual lawyer stuff. How was yours?"

"I saw the FBI agent in charge of the embezzlement case."

Melinda smiled. "I noticed you don't refer to it as the *marshmallow case* any longer."

"No," he replied. "Sarah's made that impossible."

"So what did the Feds have to say?"

"Well, I had to dance around with them."

"Proving astrology once again," said Melinda knowingly.

Lowell nodded. "Yes, I had to play that game. I read the agent's wife's birth chart and convinced him."

"No doubt," said his daughter with pride.

"Special Agent Jensen is going to do as I asked and get a forensic examiner to look over the books of the bank."

"What do you think they'll find?"

"I'm afraid they may discover a paperless trail that leads to an offshore bank."

He laughed.

"Dad?"

"I also met a Special Agent Andersen. I was just wondering if all FBI guys are *special agents*. Don't they have any *regular agents*?"

Andy drove them to the townhouse. When Melinda opened the front door Lowell's four-legged house guest welcomed her with a big wet kiss on the face.

Karen was behind him. "Luigi, stop that," she shouted. "I'm sorry, Melinda. He's just such a big baby he has to make friends with everyone."

Melinda wiped her face. "That's okay, I grew up with dogs. I'm used to being slobbered on."

Lowell came in behind Melinda. Luigi came up to him and pushed his head into Lowell's thigh. Lowell leaned over and gave him a good scratch behind the ears. "Let's sit in the living room."

Julia came out of the kitchen. "Hello Mr…David."

Lowell smiled. "Good evening, Julia."

"Dinner will be ready in about forty-five minutes. Do you need anything?"

Lowell shook his head. "No, you relax. We'll help ourselves to drinks."

Julia looked at Karen and Luigi. "He hasn't eaten yet. I've still got to make a salad. But bring him into the kitchen in a few minutes and I'll feed him." She turned back to the kitchen.

The three went into the living room and sat.

"Melinda, I want you to be ready to coordinate with me on the Williamson case. He's preparing for the operation on his twins. I expect to hear from him in a day or so, and I need to be prepared."

Lowell noticed that Karen was looking rather unhappy.

"Try not to worry," he said. "If Williamson had anything to do with your uncle's death it'll come out."

Karen bent down to rub Luigi's belly. His legs stuck up in the air. His head lay on the carpet, the tongue hanging out of the side of his mouth, a picture of total joy. "And if we don't learn the truth by the time the operation is completed, then what? You're not going to continue to investigate his death, are you?"

"Probably not," Lowell admitted.

"So then what could I do? I can't stay here much longer. Maybe I've got another day or two, but then I've got to get back to L.A. and my job."

Lowell nodded understandingly. "I'll do what I can."

Karen sighed. "I know you will. But I need closure on this, and I just won't rest until I know what happened to Uncle Mickey and why. He was like a father to me after my real dad died, and he never let me down. I don't want to let him down now."

Melinda looked over at her father's stoic face, showing little emotion. But for a slight twitch in his left eye one might have thought Karen's words had no effect. Melinda knew different. She knew this case was bringing up all sorts of emotional issues for Lowell. And she worried a bit about how it might ultimately affect him.

Lowell stretched out his legs. "Karen, there's a lot going on here that doesn't make sense. I hope that as we unravel this web of deceit, your uncle's thread will unwind as well. I've found that once the truth begins to spill out it's most difficult to stop it. I think we'll know what happened to him by the time this has all played out."

Karen stood up abruptly. Her sudden motion disturbed Luigi who got up too and watched carefully as Karen began pacing. "I can't stand feeling impotent. There's got to be something I can do. I can't just sit around waiting for you to solve this. That's just not my style."

"I don't know what else you can do," said Lowell.

"I don't know either, but I'm not sitting on my butt waiting. There's a few more leads I'm going to follow. Let's see where they take me."

"I understand your frustration. Just please be careful."

Karen grunted loudly. "I'll keep my eyes open. But remember, David, I may be short, but I'm still a cop. And I can take care of myself."

"Yes, I know you can." Lowell glanced briefly at Melinda, catching her eye. Karen noticed.

"Stop worrying. I'm not a screwball. Just an aggravated, pissed off niece." She winked at Lowell. "Who happens to carry a gun." She headed for the kitchen. "Come on, Luigi, it's supper time."

Chapter Thirty-three

Mort knocked on Lowell's office door and entered.

The detective looked up from his computer. "What have you got for me?"

Mort was on his third cup of morning coffee and talking very fast. "Neither Harriet nor her brother owns an SUV," he said, his arms waving in the air. "They both drive Toyota sedans."

"I guess it could have been a rental, or stolen," said Lowell.

"Could be. But can you prove it was them?"

Lowell shrugged. "I doubt it. But if we get them for the embezzlement it's a moot point. I'm just surprised that they would take such a big chance, especially if they hired McFarley."

"McFarley hasn't done all that well trying to eliminate you. Maybe McFarley was driving the SUV. Or maybe they just got antsy."

"I guess so. It's all down to the wire now, anyway. They know we're on to them. Now it's up to the Feds. Not much more we can do about it until we hear from them."

Jensen called at noon. "I have some news about that embezzlement. Could you possibly come to my office some time today? I want to show you the report."

"I can come right now, if that's okay. Someone seems intent on bumping me off, and I'd like it to stop as soon as possible."

"That would be fine. I'll be expecting you."

Andy dropped Lowell at the FBI headquarters.

Jensen was standing by the window looking out over New York harbor when Lowell entered. He looked over his shoulder at the detective. "Please have a seat."

Lowell sat on one of several faux leather chairs that made a semi-circle around the agent's desk. "So what have you discovered?"

The agent walked over to his desk and tossed a folder in front of Lowell. "That's the report," he said, as he sat. "Be my guest and take a look."

Lowell opened it and read through the first few pages. He closed it and put it back on the desk. "So there's nothing you can do?" he asked the agent.

Jensen shook his head. "A few days ago they moved the money into a bank in Geneva, and then wired it immediately to a bank in the Caymans. After that the trail turns cold. This guy really knows the banking business. And he had a head start. About the only chance we have of getting the money back is by grabbing them and cutting a deal."

Lowell tugged on his ponytail. "That's what I was afraid of," he said. "Suppose you did catch them, what then?"

The agent shrugged. "That depends on how willing they'd be to cooperate. I think we have enough evidence to convict, but they might be willing to sit out a long prison sentence to guarantee a comfortable old age. We'll never get the money, unless they give it up."

Lowell nodded. "It's the retirement fund for about forty employees. This is their bloodline. You think you can find them?"

Jensen smiled. "That's what we do."

"Well," said Lowell as he got up to leave, "I hope you can. I would concentrate on the airports and the docks. Neptune is quite active in their charts implying that there's a lot of water involved. I would say they're heading for an island, probably in the Caribbean."

Lowell went back to his office. Later that morning Williamson called.

"Everything's ready for the operation," he said. "Would you please call Gloria and let her know?"

"What day are you doing the procedure?"

"Day after tomorrow," said Williamson. "Friday. I'll need the boy out here the night before to prep him."

The boy, thought Lowell. *He doesn't even use his name.*

Lowell called Gloria. "Your husband is going to do the operation on Friday. You must have Kevin ready to go to the hospital tomorrow."

She was subdued and barely responded to the information.

"I'll pick you and Kevin up about noon tomorrow."

Gloria sighed audibly. "I know how busy you are, but could you possibly stay at the hospital until the operation is completed?"

"I promised you that I would be around as long as you needed me."

"Yes, you did," she replied. "And you keep your word." She sighed again. "That's a rare quality these days."

They made the arrangements and hung up.

About three o'clock Lowell's cell phone rang.

"Mr. Lowell, this is Jensen again." Lowell noticed that he didn't add his title.

"What can I do for you, Agent?"

"We caught them."

Lowell was just a bit shocked. "Already?"

"Yep," said Jensen. "We sent out their pictures over the Internet to airlines, trains, and bus stations. They were at JFK just about to board a plane to Aruba, just like you thought, when a very alert airline employee recognized them. He called us immediately and we were able to get someone there in time. They're bringing them back now. I'll be chatting with them later today. They made the mistake of thinking we wouldn't move quickly enough."

There was silence for a few moments. "We wouldn't have," added the agent, "if you hadn't forced the issue. I want to thank you."

Lowell nodded slightly, accepting the accolade graciously. "What about the money?"

"That's the rub, isn't it?" said Jensen. "We'll know a lot more once I've had time to discuss the situation with them. They're both screaming about lawyers and lawsuits, and the usual denials. Once I explain their choices, we'll see if either or both want to make a deal."

"Please let me know what you find out," said Lowell.

"Will do."

Lowell was about to hang up. "Oh, Agent Jensen, would you also try to find out if they hired McFarley and his accomplice? I'd like to put this all behind me, if possible."

"I'll let you know."

Chapter Thirty-four

The next morning Lowell was in the limo heading for the office. He was forced to forego his daily ritual walk to work much to his disappointment. Until McFarley was caught or in some way dissuaded from completing his job, caution would have to prevail.

He got into the office about seven-thirty, Starbuck's cup in hand, fed Buster and Keaton, and began his day.

The phone rang. Sarah wouldn't be in until nine, and he'd usually let it go to the machine. But things weren't usual at the moment, so he picked it up.

"Lowell."

"Mr. Lowell, this is Special Agent Jensen."

"Yes…sir," Lowell wasn't quite sure what honorific was proper.

"We've been interrogating the suspects, and I thought I'd give you an update."

"Do you need me to come in?"

"No, I can give you the gist of it over the phone."

"And what have you uncovered?" asked the detective.

"At first they both denied knowledge of the embezzlement. Said they were going on a spontaneous vacation and were completely shocked at being arrested."

"I would expect as much," said Lowell.

"But," continued Jensen, "once I showed them the evidence, they quickly changed their tune. The brother was the first to crack. When he saw the wire transfer that he had okayed, he sold his sister out in a hot minute. Said it was all her idea and that he just went along to placate her."

Lowell chuckled to himself. "What about the money?"

The agent took a moment to answer. "That's still the question. According to the bank records there was only about two million dollars transferred, but according to Buddy Ferguson there was closer to six million missing."

"That's interesting," said Lowell. "Do you think they're trying to hold on to some of it?"

"That's what we thought. We figure John Collins moved the money to several different banks, hoping to make the trail harder to follow. But only the two million went through his bank, so we're not sure what happened to the rest. I told him that a deal could be made, but only if he came clean. But he's sticking to it and the sister gave us the same exact story. Said they only took two million and she doesn't know anything about the rest. Usually if people are lying they make mistakes when we interrogate them separately and we can catch the discrepancies in their stories. But not this time."

"So now what?"

"Now," said Jensen, "we get the two million back and set our sights on the other four."

Lowell had Jensen on speakerphone and was retying his ponytail. "How long will they get?"

"In exchange for all the money, we're offering two to four years at a county facility," said the agent. "Minimum security. A country club, basically. I think they'll both take it. But if we don't get the other four million, the deal will get squashed. Then they're facing twenty years hard time."

"Let me do some work," said Lowell. "I'll get back to you."

He hung up and took out the charts for the other two employees he had originally looked at. Maybe he'd missed something. But he still didn't see anything that looked like a theft of this proportion.

At nine Sarah buzzed. Lowell buzzed back but kept working.

After about another hour he buzzed Mort.

The door opened a few moments later. "What's up, Boss?"

"I heard from Agent Jensen this morning. They've been interrogating Harriet and her brother since yesterday. According to the FBI they've admitting stealing two million dollars."

"I thought there was more than six million missing."

Lowell took a sip of coffee. "That's what Buddy told us."

"So, you'd like to know what happened to the other four million."

"Exactly."

"Okay, so what do you need from me?"

"I want you to get me the birth information for several other people at the marshmallow company." He gave Mort the names and went back to work.

An hour later Mort returned with the information. Lowell turned to his computer, entered the birth information, and punched up the astrology charts for all of the main characters in the case. He printed out the new pages and began studying each.

Mort stood over him watching. "What do you think?"

"Harriet and John Collins are crooks and they deserve to be punished. But I don't want to see them take the rap for someone else's evil deeds or see their lives irreversibly destroyed by twenty years in a federal penitentiary."

"What do you think happened to the rest of the money?"

"Someone else saw an opportunity and grabbed it."

Mort nodded. "I think you're right. Do you know who?"

"Not yet, but soon."

Lowell looked over the charts, carefully making notations on each. Then he took a single chart and circled several aspects. The rest he put into a pile and placed them in a folder. When he saw the chart of the guilty person he breathed a sigh of relief and turned to Mort with a smile.

"What do you see," asked the psychic.

"The truth," said Lowell, as he prepared to confront it.

Chapter Thirty-five

Lowell entered Buddy's office and sat down. "Where's your partner?"

"Ralph? He'll be here in a minute. What's this all about?"

"I'd rather wait until I have you both together."

A moment later the door opened and Ralph entered, still no smile. He looked out of place in this happy-go-lucky environment.

"Buddy, what's this all about? I've got a lot to do."

Buddy pointed to Lowell and shrugged. "I don't know. He wanted to see us both."

"Well, Mr. Lowell?" asked the tall, skinny man.

"The FBI grabbed Harriet and her brother."

Buddy stood up. "That's wonderful news, just wonderful. So we'll get our pension fund back?"

"Well, there's a problem," said Lowell. "They only admit to having two million of the six million you claim is missing."

Buddy sat back down. "So what, they're lying. Obviously they're trying to hold on to some of it."

Lowell shook his head. "I don't think so. I think they're both so scared of prison that they'll be willing to trade anything, including each other, to shorten their sentences. No, they would give up every dime not to do the time."

"Well," said Ralph, "then what do you think happened?"

"Someone else stole the other four million hoping Harriet and her brother would just disappear and nobody would ever notice."

Ralph sat down. "That's a fascinating theory. But who could have done that?"

"Well," said Lowell, "there aren't too many people who were in a position to do so. There was Harriet, of course. She and her brother could have moved some of the money somewhere else. But like I said, I don't think so. There are the other two suspects that you gave me when you first hired me. But I don't think either one of them did it."

Buddy was so engrossed he didn't eat a single marshmallow. "So," he asked, "who did it?"

Lowell smiled. He looked each of them in the eye. "Why, one of you two, of course."

Ralph was the first to react. "Are you kidding?" Still no smile. "Why would we?"

"Greed," said Lowell.

Ralph pointed at his partner. "Buddy, have you been a bad boy?"

"What? I didn't take it." He turned to Lowell. "What's this all about? You think I stole the money?"

Lowell shook his head. "Actually, I don't."

"Well then who…"

Lowell looked at Ralph. "Do you drive an SUV?"

"No," replied the tall, skinny man. "I drive a VW."

"Why do you want to know that?" asked Buddy.

"Someone driving a tan SUV tried to run me over the other day after I left here."

Buddy looked ill. "My sister drives a tan SUV. And he takes it to work sometimes." He turned to his brother-in-law. "Why, you rat bastard. You stole the money! How could you? Wait until my sister hears about this."

Ralph sat down, leaned back in the chair, and smiled for the first time in Lowell's presence. It wasn't a warm smile. "Wait until your sister hears about this? Your sister planned the whole thing. Once I told her that there was money missing from the pension fund, she came up with the idea of taking the rest of it."

Buddy wasn't smiling.

"Dolly was in on it?"

Ralph nodded, enjoying himself immensely.

Buddy looked pale. He was breathing heavily and holding his left arm.

"Are you alright?" asked Lowell.

Buddy turned and looked at him. "What do you think? Would you be?" He looked at Ralph with disgust. "I'll see you in jail, you thief."

Ralph leaned forward in the chair and pointed a finger at Buddy. "Yeah? Are you going to have your sister arrested too? That'd be nice. I'm sure your eighty-five-year-old mother would like that."

"You son-of-a-bitch."

"You know what you're going to do?" said Ralph. "You're going to tell the FBI that there was an accounting mistake and the four million is in another account. Then you're going to forget this ever happened."

"You better hope the old lady lives a long time. Why the fuck would you do it?"

"Because I'm sick to death of this business. Marshmallows, that's all I hear about. You stuff your face all day long with these nauseating little things. You're disgusting."

"I'm disgusting? You're a Goddamn thief and a liar."

"At least I'm not a fat little toad."

Buddy's breathing was erratic. "You're a mean, nasty man. If you ever smiled, I think your face would fall off. You look like an undertaker."

"Pig."

"Undertaker."

"Marshmallow toad."

Buddy's face grew bright red. He got up from the chair and walked around the desk. Without warning he grabbed Ralph out of his chair and threw him on the ground. Then he leaped on top of him and started pummeling him with his fists.

"You bastard!" he shouted, as he repeatedly smacked his brother-in-law in the face.

The door opened and several people who had heard the commotion entered.

"Oh my God, what's happening here?" asked the receptionist.

Buddy was slamming Ralph's head into the floor.

A few of them grabbed Buddy and pulled him off of Ralph, whose face showed the results of Buddy's attack. His nose was bleeding and his left eye was swollen shut.

Lowell stood. "I'll send you my final bill." Then he eased himself out of the office and left.

Chapter Thirty-six

Lowell's intercom buzzed.

"It's Special Agent Jensen on line one."

He picked up the phone. "Agent Jensen, what can I do for you?"

"First of all, I want to thank you for all your help with that embezzlement business."

"It was nothing."

"As you probably know, we've tied up some of the loose ends in the case. The rest of the money has been recovered."

"Yes, I know. I spoke to Buddy Ferguson."

"Yes, well, he told us that the missing six million dollars had been accidentally moved into a different account, and now he's discovered its whereabouts."

"That's what I was told."

There was silence for a few moments. Finally Jensen spoke. "Well, I'm not buying it. Nobody misplaces six million dollars and then suddenly remembers where they left it. This isn't an umbrella or a cell phone we're talking about."

Lowell tugged on his ponytail. He was hoping the agent wouldn't ask him anything that would require him to choose between lying and betraying a client's confidence. "What are you going to do about it?" he asked.

"What can I do?" Jensen sounded exasperated. "They're all sticking to that story and, well, the money's back from wherever it was. We've got Harriet and John Collins. They'll do some time, and the two million they stole is being reverted back to the U.S., so I suppose I'll have to be satisfied with that and just let it go."

"I understand."

"It's funny, though."

"What's that?" asked Lowell.

"Right after we were told that the money was found, Buddy's partner, Ralph quit the company."

"That is strange." Lowell almost held his breath.

The agent continued. "I understand he's Buddy's brother-in-law."

"That's true."

Again there was silence.

"Agent?"

"I'm just saying. Thanks for all your help. If there's anything the bureau can do for you, please let me know."

He hung up.

Mort stood by the window. "Well, that's some resolution. It was Ralph, huh?"

"Yep. He and Buddy's sister saw a chance to cash in and took it. I don't think Buddy's going to press charges. He'd have to put his sister in jail, and I don't think he's got it in him."

"So they'll get away with it, huh?"

"Well, yes and no," said the detective. "They're going to have to give back all the money if they want the Feds to stay out of it."

"And that's it?"

Lowell stood up and stretched. His right knee was bothering him. He'd have to have it looked at. "I don't know how Buddy's going to react in the long run. He obviously can't allow Ralph to stay at the company and have to deal with him everyday. But if the money is returned and he doesn't press charges, there's little the FBI can do."

"Well, I guess that case is done."

Lowell sat back down. "Now we have to concentrate on the Williamson case."

"But you found Kevin, so essentially you're done with that one, too."

"Well," said Lowell, "I've done what Williamson hired me to do. But my responsibility doesn't end there. I made a promise to his wife and I've got to keep that promise. Until the operation is completed, I've got to stick around."

"Okay, anything you need from me just let me know."

Sarah buzzed. "Melinda's on line one."

Mort headed for the door. "I'll be in my office if you need me."

Lowell put Melinda on speakerphone. "How are you?" He walked over to the turtle tank to pet his friends. Keaton looked up at Lowell, his little head nervously flitting from side to side, the red stripes on the side of his face prominent in the sunlight streaming through the window. He scratched his head and then went to his desk and sat.

"I'm okay, Dad. How are things going?"

"Well, the rest of the missing money from the marshmallow company turned up."

"Who took it?"

"Ralph."

"Oh my God. Buddy's partner?"

"Yes," said Lowell, "and Buddy's sister."

"Well that must suck for Buddy."

Lowell smiled. "Is that legalese for this type of situation?"

She chuckled. "Close enough. Is he going to press charges?"

"I don't think so."

"Can't put his family in jail, huh?"

"Yep."

"How's the other case coming along?"

"I've got to pick up Gloria and Kevin tomorrow and deliver the boy to his father. Once the operation is completed I'll be done with that business, too."

"Dad, how are you doing? I mean, really."

"Fine. Why?"

Lowell could hear Melinda fidgeting in her chair. "Oh, I don't know. It's just…"

Lowell leaned back and put his fingers on his chin. "What's bothering you?"

"Me? Why nothing."

Lowell smirked. "Oh, please. You think I can't read you? You've been acting like a mother hen since this case started."

"Well," she began slowly. "It's just that, you know, I mean, this Williamson thing is probably bringing up a lot of stuff for you."

"Well, that was clear."

"It's just that…"

Lowell interrupted her. "Let me make this easier for you. You're afraid that dealing with Williamson's children and the potential loss of one might send me off the deep end."

"Oh, I never…"

"My dear daughter, I appreciate your concern, really I do. But I'm more aware of what's going on than you think. It's been eight years since your brother passed away. And I've lived with that loss all this time. I think I'll be fine."

"Well, excuse me for caring."

"I'm very glad that you care. Please don't ever stop. I tell you what. If I start to feel weird, I'll let you know."

"Okay, Dad."

"In the meantime, you're still my attorney in this business, and until it's completed, I'll need you on your toes."

"I'm ready. Just let me know what I can do."

Lowell hung up. He sat thinking about the people he relied on and how lucky he was to have them. Sarah, Mort, Andy, and Melinda. And of course, Julia. He couldn't ask for a stronger support group.

He didn't lie to Melinda, but he admitted to himself that he'd be glad when the Williamson case was over. It was stirring some emotions more than he wanted.

Chapter Thirty-seven

Gloria opened the door and Lowell entered. There was a small suitcase sitting next to the door with a lightweight beige jacket draped across it. An iphone and ipad sat on top of the jacket.

"We'll just be a minute," said Gloria, as she hurried into the back of the apartment.

Lowell looked around at the obvious poverty, comparing it to the opulence and self-indulgence that her husband experienced every day of his life. Perhaps Williamson would be more generous now that she had acquiesced to his wishes.

Gloria returned with Kevin. He was quite tall for his age, about as tall as his father. But he still had that look of innocence that even the most precocious teenager possessed. When he saw Lowell he walked over with his hand out.

"Hey," he said, "my mom tells me that you're alright. She said you've been taking care of her. I want to thank you. That's more than my old man ever did."

Lowell shook his hand but didn't quite know how to respond.

The boy came to his rescue. "It's okay," he said with a sly smile on his face. "Didn't mean to put you on the spot. I know what my father is. He's a louse. I'm not doing this for him. I'm doing it for my brother." He picked up his iphone and punched a few buttons. Lowell figured he was checking his email. He put the phone down and looked back at Lowell. "You got a brother?"

Lowell nodded. "In fact, I do. A few years younger than me. He lives out on the West Coast."

"Would you do it? Would you give him a kidney?"

Lowell thought for a moment, then nodded. "Of course."

The kid smiled at him, then slipped earphones on his head. "That's what I thought."

Kevin headed for the door. "I'll meet you guys downstairs." He punched a button and started talking to someone named Jeanette. Then he picked up his suitcase and jacket, put his electronics in a small carrying case, and walked out.

Gloria was just checking the apartment. "I don't want to worry all night that I left the gas on or something."

"I understand," said Lowell.

She checked the stove, made sure the windows were locked, and finally turned. "Okay, I'm ready."

They went downstairs. Kevin was leaning against the limo chatting on his phone. "I'll be okay," he said. "You can text me all night. I doubt that I'll be able to sleep much." He saw Lowell and Gloria exit the building. "Jeanette, I gotta go now. I'll text you when I reach the hospital."

The three entered the limo.

"Pretty wild ride," said Kevin, as they started to drive. "It's like an office in here."

"Yes," said Lowell, "I get antsy sitting inside all day and need the freedom this allows." He pointed to his desk, complete with computer, drawers, and a swivel chair bolted to the floor of the car. "This gives me the ability to work and roam at the same time."

"Cool," said the boy nonchalantly, as he maneuvered his phone, texting and checking emails.

Lowell fiddled with the control panel. "You want to see something really cool?"

"Sure," said Kevin, without much enthusiasm.

Andy overheard and raised the barrier between the front and back seats. As Lowell turned the knobs, Kevin watched the windows darken for a moment, and then a thunderstorm in New England appeared. He put his phone down and leaned over, touching the window. It was damp and chilly, as one would expect in a cool rain storm.

"Holy crap," said the boy. "What is this?"

"It's a new type of plasma insert that a friend of mine invented."

"Are there other settings?"

Lowell pointed to the control panel. "Help yourself."

Kevin spent the rest of the trip flipping from one scenario to another, occasionally muttering a "Wow" or "Look at that!"

They arrived at Lowell's office about one o'clock. Sarah took Gloria and Kevin to the conference room, made them comfortable, and then joined Lowell in his office.

"They're okay inside for now." Sarah pushed her bright red hair back behind her ears. "He seems like a nice kid. It must be a drag to go through this at his age."

Lowell agreed. "I'm sure it's not how he planned on spending the last part of his summer vacation."

"Do you think they'll be alright?"

Lowell leaned back in his chair and put his hands behind his head. He would be happy when these two cases were over. He might even take a short vacation before jumping into the next mess. "I hope so. There's still a lot left unanswered about Williamson, but hopefully it will all go smoothly. He's supposed to be an excellent surgeon."

Sarah nodded. "What about Karen, the cop from L.A.? And what happened to her uncle?"

Lowell got up and walked to the window. He sprinkled a little food into the turtle tank and stood gazing at the New York City skyline.

"Yes, Karen's uncle. I don't know," he said as he turned back toward Sarah. "I just don't know."

Chapter Thirty-eight

Williamson arrived right on time. He entered the office and stood near the front door. "Kevin, have you packed a bag for a few days' stay?"

The boy nodded. "It's by the front door."

"Gloria," said Williamson, "I think it would be best if you didn't come right now. This will be stressful enough. I have to prep the boys for surgery, and I'll do the operation tomorrow morning. You can come out to the hospital about noon. They'll be in recovery by then."

Gloria shook her head vehemently. "I insist on coming and, at least helping Kevin settle in."

Williamson frowned. "Very well. But there's no place for you to stay."

Lowell jumped in. "Gloria, I'll have Andy drive you and Kevin out there, and once Kevin's settled in, Andy'll bring you back here."

She turned to him. "Would you?"

"I suppose that would be okay." Williamson turned toward his son. "Kevin, it's time."

Kevin stood up, his iphone in hand, rapidly texting.

Gloria walked over to him. "Did you remember to pack a toothbrush?"

"Yes Mom, I'm not a little boy anymore."

She hugged him and kissed him on the cheek.

"I know you're not."

Williamson looked at his watch impatiently and headed for the door. "Come on, it's time to go. I'll be waiting outside."

He walked out.

Kevin looked at his mother. "Try not to worry, mom. I'll be fine."

His mother looked close to tears. "I know you will."

She turned to Lowell. "I'll call you on the way back."

They left.

Lowell spent the rest of the morning sifting through his emails and phone messages trying to plan his next job. Once this business with the twins was completely resolved he would have too much time on his hands, something he loathed. He only took cases that interested him, or where he believed he could make a difference. There were a few that piqued his curiosity. He put those in his in-box. One involved the disappearance of a valuable, beloved pet tiger from a locked windowless room. He might look into that.

Gloria called in the afternoon to say she was heading back into the city. Lowell put away his work and took a short nap.

Gloria sat passively on the couch, her hands folded in her lap.

"Would you like something?" asked Lowell.

She shook her head. "No thank you." She sighed. "Well, maybe a glass of water, if you don't mind?"

Lowell went to the kitchen, opened the refrigerator, took out a Brita water pitcher and filled a glass. He walked over to the couch and handed it to Gloria.

She took a long drink. "The hospital is very nice."

"Did you see Edward?"

"Yes. But he was asleep and I didn't want to disturb him. He looked so frail and thin. I just felt so helpless."

She looked up at Lowell. Her eyes were cloudy as if in a daze. "I was so naïve and foolish when we got married." Her gaze went to the window. "Is everyone?"

"I think so."

She turned back to him. "Were you?"

He sat down and leaned back in his chair. "Yes. That may be a prerequisite for falling in love."

She nodded and turned back to the window staring at the Empire State Building. "I was so young. I thought I could be whatever he wanted me to be. And I tried very hard to live up to his expectations. But now, when I look back at it all, I realize there was nothing I could have done to make it better. He didn't want me. He wanted children. And I was only the vessel." She laughed. "Maybe he liked my genes, or my bone structure. Who knows? Everything was an experiment with him. When the boys were born he did some tests on them. A little later he came into the room and was enraged. I could see it in his face. I asked him what was wrong and he looked at me with such contempt. He shook his head and said: *You couldn't even do this right.* Then he walked out. I didn't know what he was talking about, but it scared me silly. That's when I called my sister and we started to make our plans." She shook her head. "Maybe that's when he found out that Edward had a kidney problem."

She sipped her water very carefully, her hands trembled slightly. "He'll be alright, won't he? I mean, they both will be, right?"

Lowell tugged on his ponytail. "Your husband is supposed to be an excellent doctor."

"Yes, whatever else he is, he's very good at his job."

"Well then, try not to worry too much. The operation is scheduled for tomorrow morning. My driver will take us out to the hospital by about noon and you can check on things."

She sipped her water again and nodded. "It just doesn't seem fair to put them through this at so young an age."

"I know it probably doesn't help any, but at least they have each other, and Kevin can afford to donate a kidney without it affecting his life too much."

"I know, but still, to go through this at fourteen."

"You mean fifteen."

"No, I mean fourteen. They won't be fifteen until February. You don't think a mother would forget how old her children are, do you?"

Lowell stared at her. "They weren't born June 10th, 1999?"

"That's not even close. They were born February 4th, 2000."

"February?"

"Of course. February 4th, 2000. Edward was born at 10:56 and Kevin at 11:22 in the morning in Princeton. Why?"

Lowell's face got tight. "Gloria, to the best of your knowledge does your husband know anything about astrology?"

"As a matter of fact we both were interested in it when we met. That was one of the things that we had in common. I never had any time to look into it seriously. But when we were first married he studied it extensively with someone in Manhattan. He bought dozens of books and used to go to classes at least once a week. Why do you ask?"

Lowell sat at his desk working with the Solar Fire program. He entered the new birth data for the children and drew up several charts. He worked hard not to show his concern to Gloria. He picked up the intercom and pushed a button. A few moments later there was a knock on the door. It opened and Mort entered.

"You rang?"

"Mort, this is Mrs. Williamson."

"How do you do?"

"As well as can be expected."

The strange man nodded. "I understand."

Lowell was making notes on the charts. "Mort, we have an errand to run." He turned to Gloria. "I have to take care of something. Will you be alright if I send you to your hotel?"

"I guess so. I don't really want to be alone right now. But if you must."

Lowell thought for a moment. "Let me see what I can do." He buzzed the intercom again.

Sarah entered a moment later. "Boss?"

"Sarah, please take Mrs. Williamson to the conference room and make sure she's comfortable. Then come right back."

Sarah led Gloria out the door.

Lowell turned to Mort. "I need to get a look at Edward, Williamson's sick child."

Mort was petting the turtles. "Do you think Williamson would allow that?"

"What do you think?" asked Lowell.

"So I assume we're looking at, what, five to ten for breaking-and-entering?" He laughed and flapped his elongated arms.

Lowell picked up the phone and called his daughter. "Melinda, I'm sending Mrs. Williamson to the Empire Hotel on Lexington. She's not in very good shape and I was wondering if you could get free long enough to check up on her sometime today."

"I can get out of here in about an hour," she replied. "I have to come uptown then anyway and I'll have some time in between appointments. What's going on?"

"I'll call you from the limo and explain. I may need your services in several ways before this is all over."

"That's why you paid me a retainer." She laughed.

"Okay, I'll send her to the hotel now and tell her to expect you in about an hour and a half."

They hung up. Lowell tugged on his ponytail a few times. He picked up the phone and dialed.

"Williamson Hospital."

"May I speak with Dr. Williamson please? It's David Lowell."

"I'm sorry, but the doctor just left and won't be back until tomorrow morning."

"Thank you, I'll call back then."

He called Andy. "I'm sending Mrs. Williamson down to you. Take her to the Empire Hotel and come right back."

"Gotcha, Boss."

A few moments later the door opened and Sarah entered, pad and pen in hand. "Whatcha got for me?"

"You won't need the pad. I want you to do a little extra leg-work for me."

Sarah knew what that meant, dressing up and playacting. She liked that part of it but didn't care too much for the danger it often entailed. Still, she knew that it also came with *combat pay*, and Lowell was always very generous. Sarah had a bit of a problem with shoes. She owned close to a hundred pairs that she fawned over and was always on the lookout to add to her collection. She had her eye on a pair of bright blue pumps she simply could not live without, and they cost a week's salary. This should make up for it.

"Will I need a bulletproof vest?"

"I certainly hope not," said Lowell. "It's just a reconnaissance mission."

"Okay, Boss."

Chapter Thirty-nine

The hospital was on a hill in a rural area outside Clifton, New Jersey. There was a long, winding, circular driveway that led to the big colonial mansion that housed the sanitarium. Halfway up the drive Andy stopped the limo just long enough for Lowell and Mort to jump out behind a giant azalea bush. They scurried for cover as Andy continued up the driveway.

There were few lights on the property and no visible security. Lowell and Mort were able to reach the building without being seen. Cameras were a possibility, and they kept a watch for any mounted hardware, but didn't see any. There was a locked door on the side of the hospital that took Mort less than two minutes to pick.

"How *do* you do that?"

The strange man chuckled. "I don't know. It's just obvious which way to turn the pick."

They entered the hospital through a large vacant room with a fireplace. It appeared to be a gathering place, perhaps for the staff. There was a bar and a number of couches and leather chairs. They tiptoed to the door and Lowell slowly opened it, peering out into the hallway. He checked his watch. Any second now.

Right on time, Sarah began her acting.

"What do you mean my brother isn't here?" She was shouting at the admitting nurse. "I was told he was taken to this hospital! I demand to know what's going on."

The nurse picked up the phone and a few moments later several people scurried past their door. Lowell and Mort waited a few moments, and then quickly exited the room, turned right, away from the fracas, and found an unattended staircase. They hustled up to the second floor, turned the corner, and just missed running into an intern who was hurrying down the front staircase. They waited a moment until he was out of sight.

"We only have a few minutes," said Lowell, "so let's spilt up."

Mort went to the left and Lowell to the right. They opened each door and looked in. On the third try, Mort whistled a low, brief tweet. Lowell rushed over.

"He's in here," Mort whispered.

They quietly entered the room closing the door behind them. It was nicely furnished, with bright curtains and several comfortable chairs. The late afternoon sun poured through the half-opened curtains casting eerie shadows on the walls. There was a large, flat-screen TV on the wall that was turned off, and a number of flower bouquets and get-well cards on the dresser. Except for a graphic novel for teens that sat on the night table, and a poster of a young female singer Lowell didn't recognize, there was little to interest a teenager.

In the bed lay the boy. Lowell walked over to him. His eyes were closed, and he seemed asleep. He looked to weigh perhaps eighty-five pounds. Although he was gaunt and pale, his features were so much like his brother Kevin's it was unsettling. Lowell thought he looked like a Xerox copy that didn't come out quite right. He had IVs in both arms and was attached to an elaborate mechanism that beeped every few moments. There was a monitor with a continuously moving line that would jump every couple of seconds. Lowell stared at it, momentarily mesmerized. Then he shook his head.

"I want some pictures," he said, motioning to Mort. "Get some shots of him and these devices he's hooked up to."

Mort took out a small digital camera and took several shots of the boy and the machines he was hooked up to. It took only a few minutes to complete the process. When he was done, Mort put the camera into his pocket and nudged Lowell.

Having seen what he came to see Lowell turned to leave when a frail voice stopped him.

"Who are you?"

Lowell turned to face the boy. "I just came by to see how you were doing."

"Oh. Are you a doctor?"

"No, just someone who's concerned."

The boy nodded, and then closed his eyes once more and fell back asleep.

As they sneaked out of the room they could hear Sarah wailing. They ran down the same staircase and out the side door, carefully staying in the shadows when possible. Lowell took out his cell phone and dialed Sarah.

"It's okay," he said, "we're done."

"Yes mother…You mean to tell me you sent me to the wrong hospital? Do you know how upset I've been and how much trouble I've caused these good people?…Alright I'm on my way there now."

She hung up and turned to the admitting nurse.

"I'm so dreadfully sorry for this terrible mix up. It appears my brother was taken to a hospital a few towns over. Please accept my apologies."

The nurse frowned and nodded—her displeasure quite apparent.

Sarah hurried out of the hospital to the waiting limousine and jumped into the back. Andy slowly drove her down the driveway, stopping once again by the azaleas to pick up the boys.

Chapter Forty

The sun was just approaching the horizon when they got back to the office. Twilight would be in about half an hour. The late summer sun cast an otherworldly red hue about the city making it look like an artist's rendition of Mars on the cover of a nineteen sixties Ray Bradbury paperback.

Lowell took out his keys and opened the door to the Starlight Detective Agency. Sarah went in first and turned on the light on her desk. She was followed by Mort and Lowell.

"Mort, would you download those pictures for me now?"

Mort nodded emphatically. He took the digital camera from his pocket. "I can do it easier on your computer." He started walking toward Lowell's private office. "David, have you got a beer? I'm dying of thirst."

"In the fridge in my office. I'll have one too."

"Sarah?"

"Sure. I'd love a cold one. Let me check the machine for messages."

Lowell waved his hand. "Forget it. Do it in the morning. Let's just relax for a few minutes. That was an exhilarating experience."

Sarah smiled. She liked working for Lowell. He was kind and smart, and paid her twice what she could make anywhere else. Besides, where else could she dress up and play private eye games?

Mort entered the inner office and turned on the overhead light. "Oh my God. David, get in here!"

Lowell and Sarah hurried through the door. Mort pointed to the safe. The Modigliani print was lying on the ground and the door of the safe was ajar. "You were robbed."

Sarah gasped. "The million dollars."

Mort turned toward her. "That's right. It was here."

The redhead nodded silently. "A million dollars!" She turned to Lowell. "What are you going to do?"

Lowell didn't seem all that upset. He tugged on his ponytail and shrugged. "There's nothing much I can do."

Sarah looked downright miserable. "What do you mean? There's got to be something you can do."

Lowell sat behind his desk, leaned back in the chair, retied his ponytail and smiled a sly grin.

Mort looked at him for a moment. "You moved it, didn't you?"

His smile widened.

Sarah pushed her hair out of her face. "You did? How did you know?"

"There's just something so wrong about this whole affair that's made me more guarded. There's a nasty aspect happening in the sky right now. Uranus, the ruler of sudden events is in square to Pluto, the planet of vengeance and hidden agendas, and that square is being set off right now by the Sun and Mars. I thought it would be prudent to use some extra caution, so I took the money to the townhouse last night. The security system there is much better."

Sarah sank into the couch. "Well, thank God that you did." She took off her shoes and rubbed her feet. "Now I can really use that beer. This has been one hell of a day."

Sarah went to the small kitchen and prepared the drinks and then sat back on the couch. She raised her chilled glass. "Here's to a million bucks and the smartest detective in New York."

Mort laughed. "Here, here." They clinked their glasses together and each took a sip. "Are you going to tell Lieutenant Roland about the break in?"

Lowell shook his head. "I wouldn't want to go through the hassle. There's nothing they can do about it anyway. And we

didn't lose the money. Frankly, I would just as soon not discuss
the briefcase and its contents until I see how this case works out.
Have either of you mentioned it to anyone?"

They both shook their heads.

"Good. Let's keep it that way."

Mort took a slug of beer. "I know the world's gone crazy and
things aren't worth what they used to be. But that's still a lot of
money to me."

Sarah smiled strangely. "Do you know how many pairs of
shoes I could buy with a million bucks?" She stared off into
space imagining row after row of Steve Maddens.

"Who do you think did it?" asked Mort.

Lowell did not look happy. "There was only one person
outside of us who knew I had it."

Sarah nodded. "Williamson."

Lowell tugged on his ponytail. "Exactly."

"But why would he have someone try to steal it back?"

"I don't know. Maybe they were really looking for the computer files Karen's uncle sent. And maybe the million dollars was
just the carrot for the jackass that he hired to do this."

Sarah swigged her beer. "That's some carrot."

Lowell nodded.

"Well," said Mort, "they didn't get it."

"No," said Lowell, "they didn't. But that may not stop them
from trying again. Hopefully this will all be cleared up tomorrow. In the meantime, Mort download those pictures. I'm going
to need them right away. And Sarah, get me Dr. Martin Reed.
You'll find his number in my files."

Chapter Forty-one

Sarah took her beer back to her desk. A few minutes later the intercom buzzed. Lowell picked it up.

"I've got Dr. Reed on line one."

"Martin, it's David Lowell."

"David, how nice to hear from you. Nothing serious I hope."

"Well, that depends upon your point of view. I'm fine."

"Is it Melinda?"

"No, thank God. It's about a client. I was wondering if you could look at some pictures and tell me what's wrong with the patient."

"I don't know until I've seen them. What's this about?"

"I'd rather tell you in person. I know it's getting late. Do you have any time today?"

"Just a minute, let me check my schedule."

He put Lowell on hold. Insipid elevator music played: "You Light up My Life." Lowell put the phone on speaker and turned it down. Of all the annoying things in society, and this was very near the top of his list.

After a few minutes Dr. Reed returned.

"David, are you there?"

Lowell picked up the phone. "I'm here."

"Good. I thought the music might have been too much for you."

Lowell laughed. "I almost gave up."

"Terrible, isn't it? I've tried to get them to remove it, but everyone in the office tells me that without it people will think we've hung up on them. I'm pretty much done for the day. I've got some paperwork to take care of and then I'm heading home. But I'll be here for a little while. I can see you in about thirty minutes. Does that work?"

"I'll be there. Thank you, Martin."

Lowell hung up and called Andy, who was waiting downstairs with the limo when Lowell exited the building. They nodded to each other as he got into the back of the car.

"Bellevue Hospital, Andy."

"Having problems, Boss?"

"Yes, but nothing a little Prozac couldn't clear up."

"Shall I wait, or are you checking in?"

Lowell laughed.

Andy drove up First Avenue and pulled over at the hospital entrance. Lowell got out in front of the storied building.

"I shouldn't be long. They'll probably make you move. I'll text you when I'm ready to leave."

He entered the hospital, took the elevator to the fourth floor, and entered Reed's office. He walked to the receptionist's desk.

"David Lowell to see Dr. Reed."

"He's expecting you. Go right in."

When Lowell entered the office Reed was sitting behind his desk looking over some x-rays. When he saw Lowell, he stood and extended his hand.

"David, how nice to see you. You're looking well." He looked at Lowell's slight paunch. "Maybe too well." He laughed.

They sat.

"Ah, the good life," said Lowell, patting his belly. "How's Barbara?"

"She's great. She started teaching again at NYU Medical Center and loves it. We're running away for a week to Barbados at the end of September. I can't wait. I haven't had a vacation in two years."

Lowell smiled knowingly.

"You too?" asked Reed.

Lowell nodded. "Closer to four years, I think."

"Well, it's time you got away. When Barbara hears that I saw you, she'll have a dozen questions. How's Melinda? Do you get to see much of her?"

"Actually I do, lately. In fact I've hired her to help out on a case. She's doing quite well in her law career and seems to be healthy and happy."

"You're lucky. If I see my kids twice a year it's a lot. One lives in Boston and the other lives in south Jersey. But they're always busy. Grandkids and all, you know how it is."

"Not really," replied Lowell, "but I can imagine."

Reed nodded understandingly. "Melinda's still single?"

"Yeah, I keep hoping she'll find someone."

"Well," said Reed, "I've known her since she was about five. She always was very independent, even as a child. And a bit of a tomboy."

Lowell smiled at his old friend. "Yes, that's my little girl."

"Little?" Reed chuckled. "She was taller than you when she was eleven."

Lowell laughed.

"So," said the doctor, "tell me, what's this all about?"

Lowell took the pictures from his pocket and handed them to Reed. "Can you tell me what these machines are?"

Reed looked at the pictures for a few moments. "Where did these shots come from?"

"A private hospital in New Jersey. Why?"

"This boy is very sick."

"I know that. But what's wrong with him? Is it his kidneys?"

"Kidneys? No, this isn't a dialysis machine he's hooked up to."

"Then what is it?"

He told Lowell.

"That's what I was afraid of," said the detective.

"Of course, without seeing the patient and his records," continued Reed, "I can't make a definitive diagnosis. But I'm pretty sure. How old is he?"

"Fourteen."

"How sad. Do you know if there's a donor?"

A chill went through Lowell. "Yes, I believe there is. Can you tell me what the risks are?"

"With any transplant most of the problems have to do with the body rejecting the new organ."

"So I've been told. Who would be most compatible?"

"Family members are the best, although with any transplant, the recipient would still need to take immune suppressant drugs, probably for the rest of his or her life."

Lowell nodded. "How about an identical twin?"

Dr. Reed stroked his chin and smiled. "That would be a surgeon's dream come true. The DNA of the two is identical and the body wouldn't reject the new organ. Most likely the patient wouldn't even need the drugs."

"And if one of the twins had a rare blood type?"

"The other would have the same blood type. There shouldn't be any discrepancy at all."

Lowell sat quietly for a moment. He glanced at the many degrees and various framed awards and other accolades that adorned the office walls. His old friend was one of the most highly acclaimed surgeons in America. Lowell had gotten the confirmation he'd expected, which complicated things greatly.

Dr. Reed sat patiently for a few moments. Finally he spoke. "Is this your client?"

"More or less," said the detective. "It's one of the parents."

The doctor nodded knowingly. "It seems to me that you've got a difficult road ahead of you."

Lowell stood. "Goes with the territory."

"Yes," said Reed. "In a way our jobs aren't that different. People only come to us when they're in trouble."

Reed got up and walked Lowell to the door. "Let me know if there's anything else I can do for you."

"Thank you, Martin, you've been invaluable. Please give my regards to Barbara and the boys."

Chapter Forty-two

When Lowell was back in the limo he made a call.

"Melinda, I think we've got a much bigger problem than I realized. I need you to do some work ASAP on who has legal rights in the medical decisions of the children of estranged parents."

"What's going on, Dad? What do you need specifically?"

Lowell's mind was racing. He had to make it in time. "Can a parent prevent a medical procedure if he or she believes it will harm their child? And what if one parent wants to do it and the other doesn't?"

"Okay, hold on a second."

He heard her buzz her intercom and talk to her legal aide. "Victor, I need all the information you can get regarding parental rights in a medical emergency. Concentrate on estranged parents who disagree on the procedure…Hold on one second."

She came back on the line. "Dad, I assume this is in New Jersey?"

"Yes."

"Okay, hold again…Victor, focus on New Jersey laws."

"Okay, Dad, I'm back. Now what's going on?"

"You have the Solar Fire software installed in your office computer?"

"Yes," said his daughter.

"Good. I want you to punch in two birth dates."

"Okay, what names go on the charts?"

"Edward Williamson. Both of them." He gave her the dates and times, and then he waited. He could hear her fingers clicking on the keyboard.

After a minute or so she said "I've got them both here. One is the birth information of the boy we looked at last week. What's the other one?"

"The other is the boy's real birth information."

"You mean Williamson lied to you? Why would he do that?"

"Melinda, do you remember the diagnosis we made for Edward?"

"Of course. He has advanced kidney disease."

"And you remember how we made that diagnosis?"

"Certainly," she said. "You always said medical interpretation was one of the most important things in astrology and drummed it into my head pretty good. Venus is afflicted by Neptune and the Moon, which showed a propensity toward kidney disease of some sort. You didn't seem surprised at that."

"Nor should I be. Now, look at the second chart."

He heard her rustling papers as she looked over the chart with the new birth information Gloria had provided.

"Dad, this is a different date. And even a different year. What's this all about?"

"What do you see in the chart?"

"Well, Venus is in square to Saturn, but it's not nearly as afflicted as in the other chart you showed me."

"No, it isn't."

"He might be socially awkward or uncouth in some ways," said Melinda, "and there could be kidney stones, but that's about all. There aren't enough negative aspects to point toward life threatening kidney problems. But another planet is besieged in this chart."

"Exactly. And what does that other planet rule in medical astrology?"

She told him.

"You always were my best student." His pride was obvious.

"What does this mean?" she asked.

"It means that I've been duped," said the astrologer. "And if I don't hurry, a terrible injustice is about to occur."

"You don't think..." she stopped. "Oh my God. That would be monstrous. You can't be serious."

"I have never been more serious about anything in my life."

"What are you going to do?"

Lowell leaned forward in his chair. "I'm going to stop him. There's nothing I can do tonight. Williamson's not at the hospital. I'll have to wait until the morning."

Melinda blew out a large breath of air. "What can I do?"

"You can earn your retainer. Just keep your phone near you and on at all times. I may need your services at any moment. I'll contact you. Did you go see Mrs. Williamson?"

"Yes, she's resting at the hotel."

"Good. Melinda, I need you to be up and alert very early tomorrow morning. There's nothing I can do right now, but it's imperative that we coordinate this all tomorrow."

"I'll be ready."

He hung up. "Andy, drive me to the office."

Lowell then called Gloria and told her to be ready to leave the next morning at five-thirty.

"Five-thirty? Why so early?"

"I think it would be best."

Chapter Forty-three

The next morning Lowell woke at four, showered and dressed, and was in the limo before five. When they got to the hotel he ran into the lobby and found Gloria sitting quietly in an armchair near the elevators.

When she saw Lowell she stood up suddenly and rushed toward him. "Can you tell me why we have to be there so early? Has something gone wrong?"

Lowell shook his head. *Not yet, I hope*, he thought.

She followed him out the hotel entrance and into the limo.

Andy had the radio tuned to 1010 WINS so he could hear the traffic report every ten minutes. He turned around toward Lowell. "The Lincoln Tunnel outbound is backed up. Tractor-trailer jack-knifed and it's a long wait. As of right now, the Holland Tunnel's the best bet. But it could bottle-up at any minute. We could go up to the GW Bridge, but that might take an extra hour in travel time."

"What do you think?" asked Lowell.

"I'd take a chance on the Holland if we can get there soon."

"Do it."

Andy expertly maneuvered the limo through early pre-rush hour mid-town traffic, zipping through spaces only inches wider than the car. Getting across town wasn't a problem. But when they reached the west side they could already see the cars backed-up going into the Holland Tunnel. Usually at this time of day leaving the city would be a snap, but the accident in the Lincoln Tunnel would screw things up for hours at all the Hudson River crossings.

They got through the tunnel in about thirty minutes. Lowell kept glancing nervously at the time on his phone.

He called Melinda at six. "Are you awake?"

"Yes, Dad," said a grumpy voice, "I'm up. Where are you?"

"We just got out of the Holland Tunnel in Jersey. We should be at the hospital in about thirty minutes. Are you ready?"

"Yep." She yawned. "Got all the right stuff in front of me."

"Well, let's see how this goes. If I need you, I'll call."

He hung up.

◇◇◇

Andy drove the limo up to the front of the hospital. Lowell exited, extending his hand toward Gloria who took it and stepped from the car.

She looked up at the three-story colonial mansion that housed her husband's private laboratory and shivered at the wealth and power it represented.

Lowell turned to Andy "If you don't hear from me in thirty minutes, you know what you have to do."

Andy nodded. "I'm ready."

Lowell and Gloria went up the white wooden steps onto the wraparound porch, and entered the building. The admitting nurse at the front desk looked up as they entered. "May I help you?"

"This is Mrs. Williamson, Dr. Williamson's wife."

The nurse looked at Gloria suspiciously. "I didn't know the doctor was married."

"We've been separated for many years."

The nurse eyed her for a moment. "How can I help you?"

"Mrs. Williamson needs to see her husband immediately," said Lowell. "It's a matter of the gravest importance."

"Well, this is most irregular." The nurse picked up the phone and pushed several numbers. "There's a woman here claiming to be Dr. Williamson's wife...I didn't know either...Well could you check for me please?" She hung up. "It'll be a few moments. The doctor is prepping for surgery."

"I'm sure he is," said Lowell.

A moment later the phone rang. The nurse picked it up. "Yes? I see. Alright, thank you." She hung up. "Someone will be right down."

A nurse came down the winding staircase. "Mrs. Williamson?"

Gloria nodded.

"Would you please come this way?"

Gloria and Lowell began to follow her.

"I was only told to bring Mrs. Williamson, nobody else."

Lowell was about to protest when out of the corner of his eye he spotted him. At first it was too quick a glance to be sure. Precious seconds passed. Finally he saw him again, clearly this time, his reflection in the hall mirror as he hid behind the door, his scar quite visible. McFarley.

Lowell tensed, expecting trouble. "I'm here as Mrs. Williamson's adviser, and I must insist."

Lowell looked in the mirror again but McFarley was gone.

The nurse shrugged. "I have to clear it."

She walked over to the admitting desk and whispered a few words to the nurse who picked up the phone, hit some buttons, and whispered into it. Then she nodded.

"Very well, follow me." She headed up the stairs with Lowell and Gloria right behind.

They were led into a comfortable waiting room with several couches and chairs all made of expensive looking leather. There were two very large windows overlooking the expansive grounds. It was a beautiful clear day with just a wisp of white clouds hanging in the sky. One window was open allowing in a gentle late summer breeze. Lowell noted the faint smell of chrysanthemum blossoms.

"If you will wait here. I'll get the doctor."

They sat.

Gloria's nervousness was obvious. She kept wringing her hands as if trying to wash off some horrible stain. "I just know something's terribly wrong."

Lowell patted her shoulder. "Try to relax. We'll get to the bottom of this."

The door to the operating room opened and Williamson came through it. "Now, what's this all about? For God's sake, I'm about to perform a lifesaving operation, as you know. Can't this wait?" He was dressed in dark green scrubs, holding a pair of latex gloves, a surgical mask hanging off his ears. He impatiently smacked the gloves against his left hand as he spoke.

Lowell stood and stepped toward Williamson. "I'm afraid not. You lied to me about your sons' birth information."

"What? What is this nonsense?"

"You gave me the wrong date and year of birth."

"Mr. Lowell, I have a serious task at hand. I can't be bothered with some triviality. Perhaps I made a mistake, or maybe you misheard me."

Lowell shook his head. "It was no mistake. You know a great deal more about astrology than you let on. Your wife tells me that you spent several years studying the celestial arts."

"Well, yes, that's true. I didn't want you to think that I might challenge your results or second guess you, so I kept that to myself."

"You also studied with Jeannie McMillan, whose specialty is medical astrology."

"I'm a doctor. And you of all people should understand my interest in the subject."

"I most certainly do. The first chart you gave me showed a weakness in the kidneys. The real birth chart shows the difficulty is in another part of the body."

Williamson shrugged. "So you say. I don't agree."

Lowell smiled briefly. "I thought you didn't want to challenge my expertise."

Williamson wasn't easily intimidated. "Perhaps in this case you've made a mistake."

"Perhaps." Lowell gestured toward his garb. "You're prepared for the transplant?"

"Yes, if you'll let me do my job."

"Alone?"

"Of course not. No transplant can be done solo. I've called in Dr. Lewis Meltzer to assist in the operation. He's the top man in his field and will be invaluable in case something were to go wrong."

"What could go wrong?" asked Lowell.

Williamson was obviously annoyed. "There are always unknown factors in every operation. Dr. Meltzer is one of the top transplant surgeons in the country. He has performed count-less kidney operations and has the highest degree of success."

"Does he only do kidney transplants?"

Williamson remained silent.

Gloria looked at Lowell. "What's going on?"

"Your husband purposely gave me the wrong birth informa-tion for your twins."

He turned to Williamson. "You told me that Edward was born June 10th, 1999, at 3:44 a.m., fourteen minutes after Kevin. This chart shows a very afflicted Venus, ruler of the kid-neys. You knew I would interpret the chart that way and cleverly chose that birth date and time so I wouldn't suspect your true motivations. In fact, Edward was born February 4th, 2000 at 10:56 in the morning, twenty-six minutes before Kevin. This gives him a Sun-Uranus conjunct in square to Saturn and the ascendant. Venus isn't afflicted in this chart at all. It's the Sun that's badly placed. And because of the time difference of twenty six minutes, the ascendant, which rules the physical body, is only part of that equation in Edward's chart, not Kevin's. That's why Edward has developed the problem and not his brother."

Gloria looked confused, and scared. "What does all of this mean?"

Lowell looked at Williamson. "Do you want to tell her, or shall I?"

"Tell me what?"

Williamson said nothing.

"The Sun in an astrology chart rules the heart and circulatory system. Uranus is the most upsetting and erratic of the planetary influences."

Lowell took a step toward Williamson. "The machine your son is hooked up to. Tell her," he pointed to Gloria. "Tell her what it is."

Gloria was shaking. "What is it?"

Lowell could hardly contain his anger. "It's an external ventricular assist device or VAD. It's used to replace the function of a failing heart. I'd say that Edward is in the final stages of heart disease."

Williamson's face was stone.

Lowell was enraged. "Gloria, your son doesn't need a kidney transplant. He needs a new heart."

"What?" asked Gloria. It still hadn't sunk in. "What are you talking about? A heart transplant, but that's impossible. For that to happen he'd have to…" her voice trailed off as the reality hit her.

Lowell turned to Dr. Williamson. "Did you plan to have an accident occur during the operation that would kill Kevin, but still give yourself time to make the switch? Maybe too much anesthesia with the help of Maria Rodriguez?"

Williamson's stoic persona was starting to crumble. He slowly moved to his left.

Lowell looked at Gloria. "He planned to take Kevin's heart and put it into Edward."

Gloria's eyes grew wide. She leaped out of the chair and shrieked. "What! Why you bastard. How could you kill your own son?"

Williamson strode quickly over to the desk before Lowell could react, opened the drawer, and removed a pistol. He whirled around and pointed it at Lowell. "Kevin isn't my son. He stopped being so the day you took him away from me. Edward is my only child, and I will do whatever it takes to save him." He reached into the desk drawer and removed a silencer, which he slowly screwed onto the end of the gun as he talked.

He waved the gun at Lowell and started to pace. Gloria held onto Lowell's arm for support. "Don't be a hero, or I'll use this. No matter the consequences, I'm going to do this operation. My son, Edward, is not going to die."

Lowell stared at him, helpless to act. He fisted his right hand in futile anger, then relaxed it, and took a deep breath. Unfocused fury never got you anywhere. "You had McFarley kill that private eye in L.A., didn't you? He found out that you illegally acquired some of your patents."

Williamson shrugged. "What could they prove? That was just a nuisance. My lawyers would have taken care of that."

Lowell nodded. Maybe if he could keep him talking an opening would present itself. "That's what I thought. So what happened? Did he also uncover the plan you had for your sons?"

Williamson turned his head slightly. "That detective was too smart for his own good. Once he discovered that Gloria was living on the East Coast he wouldn't leave it alone, even after I paid him off and told him to drop it. He had to keep digging."

"So you had him killed."

"I admit to nothing. You've got no proof."

"What do you think you're going to do with us?"

Williamson picked up the phone and pushed a few numbers. "McFarley, get up to the third floor, outside operating room number two. And bring your gun."

He hung up.

"He's on his way," Williamson sneered at Lowell, "and then I will proceed with the operation. If either of you interferes I'll have you killed."

"You can't get away with it," Lowell replied in a clear, steely voice. His powerless rage bubbled just below the surface.

"These walls are very thick, almost soundproof. I don't believe a gunshot with a silencer would be heard." Williamson glanced behind him at the open window and edged his way over to it. "I don't want to kill you, but I will if necessary. I'll just say that she became hysterical, you reacted violently, and I was forced to protect myself. Without a witness, and with you both dead, it'll be my word alone. And in any case, no matter what happens to me, my son will be alive."

Williamson slowly backed up, his attention never straying from Lowell, the gun never wavering. He reached the open window, shifting his eyes briefly, put one hand on the open window, and was about to close it.

Gloria screamed: "You son of a bitch. You're not killing my boy." She shoved off Lowell and leaped the two steps toward Williamson, landing in front of him. There was no time for Lowell to react.

By the time Williamson realized what was happening, it was too late. He started to turn the gun in her direction. Her eyes were wild with rage, her breathing erratic. She smacked both hands onto his chest, driving the gun hand up and shoving him at the open window. She spit as she shouted: "No, you bastard!"

Off balance, trying to angle for a shot, he stumbled back as Gloria butted her head, shoulders, and open hands into him with the strength of a mother lion protecting her cub. The gun flew out of his hands as he tried to grab hold of the wooden window frame, fingers scrabbling. His hand slipped off the slick wood as Gloria heaved with all her scrawny might, grunting, wild with rage, and toppled him out the window. They could hear his scream all the way down followed by a sickening distant *thump*.

Gloria dropped to the floor shaking violently. Lowell ran to her and cradled her in his arms. "It's over, it's alright."

He kicked the gun under the desk just as the door opened and a nurse appeared. She stared at Lowell and Gloria for a few moments.

Lowell looked up at her. "We need some help here."

"I'll get the head nurse." She quickly left the room.

Lowell stood and scooped up the gun using a tissue, careful not to leave any prints, put it back in the desk drawer, and then went back to Gloria and wrapped his arms around her. The door opened and several people came in, including McFarley.

The head nurse entered. "What's happened here?" she bellowed.

Gloria started to speak. "I…"

"There's been a terrible accident," said Lowell. "Dr. Williamson went over to close the window and tripped."

The nurse looked out the open window. There were several people surrounding Williamson's body. "Oh my dear, God!" She turned to another nurse. "Olivia, please call the police."

Lowell saw McFarley hurry out.

The nurse picked up the phone. "This is Nurse Johnson. What's the status on Dr. Williamson?...I see...Let me know when the police arrive." She hung up and turned toward Gloria. "Your husband is dead. He landed on his head and apparently died instantly."

Gloria fainted into a heap.

Chapter Forty-four

Lowell picked up Gloria and carried her to the couch. The nurse took her pulse on her wrist and neck.

Gloria began to come around. "What happened?"

"You fainted," said the nurse. "Can you sit up?"

"I think so."

With Lowell's help she managed to get into a seated position. The nurse handed her a glass of water and applied a wet cloth to her forehead.

Gloria sipped the water. "I'm feeling much better, thank you." Color was starting to return to her face.

The door to the operating room opened and a man wearing scrubs and gloves came out. "What's going on here?"

The nurse walked over to him. "Dr. Meltzer, there's been a terrible accident. It's Dr. Williamson. He's fallen out the window. I'm afraid he's dead."

"What?" said Meltzer, the shock quite obvious on his face. "Dead? But how is that possible? Who was here when it happened?"

"We were." Lowell extended his hand.

The doctor took off his glove and shook it, without thinking. "Who are you?"

"David Lowell. I'm a private detective hired by Dr. Williamson to find the whereabouts of his wife."

"Wife? I didn't even know Edgar was still married."

Gloria sat forward. "I'm Mrs. Williamson. We've been apart for many years but never divorced."

Meltzer sat in one of the chairs. "I don't know what to say. Edgar was my friend. I just can't believe this has happened."

Lowell took Gloria's hand and patted it. She smiled weakly. The door to the operating room opened again and a young woman in scrubs came out sobbing. As she ran past, Dr. Meltzer called out. "Maria?" But she continued out the door of the waiting room.

Lowell watched. "Maria Rodriguez, I assume?"

"That's right," said Meltzer. "But how…"

"I don't think she's coming back."

"I don't understand."

Lowell turned to the doctor. "I'll explain it all to you in due time. Right now we have another problem that must be addressed immediately. There's a very sick boy in that operating room."

The doctor looked at him, his attention scattered. "Yes, I was about to assist in a transplant."

"Doctor, what are the options for a heart transplant when a potential donor dies suddenly?"

The doctor sat back in the chair and removed the second glove. "While other organs such as kidneys can be kept ready for some time, a heart transplant must occur within about four hours of the removal of the organ."

"Dr. Williamson was an organ donor. You'll find that in his records."

Meltzer shook his head. "The closest transplant center is in New York. We would have to hurry to secure Dr. Williamson's organs, especially the heart, to make sure it can be donated in time."

"You have a patient right here who's on the list of recipients, but without a proper donor."

Dr. Meltzer looked surprised. "But I don't understand."

Lowell tugged on his ponytail and tried to word his response carefully. "Actually, if you examine the donor you'll find that he's a perfectly healthy young man."

The doctor looked at him incredulously. "What are you talking about? I was told the boy had late stage brain cancer with very little time left. I have to look into this."

He went into the operating room and returned a few minutes later.

"I don't know what's going on here, but I was brought in to assist in a heart transplant, and now I find that my donor is, in fact, perfectly healthy. This is most irregular."

"I believe you will find Dr. Williamson's blood type is a match for his son. Can you do the operation?"

"I can. But I don't know if I should. There's something very amiss here."

Gloria stood unsteadily, walked over to him and took his hand. "My boy is dying. Without this transplant he won't last much longer. He's on the list of recipients, and his father is a donor."

Meltzer went to the computer and opened a file. "Yes, I see that the boy has been on the list of recipients for the last year. But I'm not sure about the legality of all of this."

Lowell took out his cell phone. "Perhaps I can help."

He called Melinda. "It's me. I'm at the hospital in New Jersey and there's been a terrible accident. Dr. Williamson fell out of a window and is dead. I have Dr. Meltzer here and I need you to talk to him. We need to transplant Williamson's heart into his son Edward as soon as possible, and there may be some legal problems you should discuss with Dr. Meltzer. The boy's mother is here and prepared to okay the operation."

He handed the phone to Meltzer. After a brief conversation and a number of *grunts* and *I sees*, he handed the phone back to Lowell.

Meltzer turned to Gloria. "And you're his mother?"

"Yes."

"And you agree to this operation?"

"Absolutely."

"Well, this is most…fortuitous." He picked up the phone and pushed two numbers. "Get me Dr. Williamson's medical records and a release form for a heart transplant STAT. And I need someone who can assist in a transplant." He was about to hang up. "Oh, and get me an anesthesiologist."

He hung up. "You know there is no guarantee that his body will accept the new heart, although being a parent increases the chances that the HLA markers will match. The boy's chest cavity appears to be large enough to accommodate his father's heart." He turned toward Gloria. "Even if the operation is successful your boy will probably have to take autoimmune drugs for the rest of his life."

Gloria nodded.

"They're very expensive," said the doctor.

She sighed. "I hadn't thought of that."

Lowell took her hand. "Please don't worry about that now. One thing at a time. Let's just get through this procedure."

Another nurse brought up the necessary paperwork for Gloria's signature.

Dr. Meltzer went into the operating room and returned about fifteen minutes later. He shook his head. "I'm not completely satisfied that everything is on the up and up. I don't know what's going on. It isn't like Edgar to make such a grievous mistake. But I've seen the medical situation, and that boy in there desperately needs a new heart soon or he will die. His father has suddenly become a donor, and there is nothing else I can do but perform this operation. The blood work shows compatibility and there is every possibility that it will be successful." He headed toward the scrub room. "Now if you'll forgive me I have a transplant to see to."

Chapter Forty-five

The operation was a success. Edward was in recovery and doing well when Lowell and Melinda came in the next day.

Gloria and Kevin were sitting in the waiting room. She stood and walked over to Lowell.

"May I speak with you over here for a moment?" she asked.

They walked over to the window. The hospital grounds were vast, with rows of trees and roaming meadows spread out over a dozen acres. *To have a backyard like this,* thought Lowell.

Gloria took his arm. "I haven't told Kevin about how his father died."

Lowell nodded.

"I was wondering if you had any advice. I mean, how do I tell my boys that I killed their father?"

Lowell sighed. "You didn't kill him. It was an accident. You didn't set out to do him harm, you just reacted to the situation. I don't think you ever do tell the boys about your part in it. I know it's going to be difficult to live with this hanging over your head for the rest of your life, but truthfully, what would be the point? It would upset them both and do nothing to change the situation."

"But…" she began.

Lowell held up his hand. "Only you and I know what happened. I've told my daughter, but she was acting as council and anything I said is attorney-client privilege and will never be repeated. You did what you had to do to save your child's life.

Things occurred because of your husband's actions and it is his karma that they turned out the way they did. The spiritual bank books had to be balanced, and your husband's transplanted heart kept your children alive and your family together. There's nothing to be gained by confessing now, except a somewhat selfish desire to cleanse yourself of something that doesn't need cleansing. This will all work itself out through the years and future lifetimes."

"It will be hard. I'm a very honest person."

"I know," said the astrologer. "But who would benefit from it? If you were removed from the home, these boys wouldn't have a parental figure to help them as they enter adulthood. They both will need you very much, Edward especially."

She nodded. "I suppose you're right."

Then she dropped her hands into her lap. She looked down at them, seeming quite sheepish once again after her burst of strength and conviction the day before. "I don't know how I'm going to raise them. Edward's medication is terribly expensive, even if I can get health insurance."

"First things first. Get Edward on the road to recovery and then we'll deal with everything else. I want you to come to my office in a few days." He motioned to Melinda. "I'd like you to talk to my daughter for a few moments."

Melinda walked over. "Mrs. Williamson, how are holding up?"

"Gloria, please. I…I don't know how I'm holding up, to be honest. This has all been so much to take in. Until a few weeks ago, I hadn't seen my husband or my other son for almost fifteen years. Now I suddenly I have my boy back with me. And Edgar is…"

She closed her eyes and shuddered. "Oh, I'll never forget that moment when I realized that he meant to take my Kevin's life." She opened her eyes and looked at Lowell. "No, I won't tell the boys what happened. You're right. I did exactly what I had to do. Sometimes it's just that clear, isn't it?"

"Sometimes," said Lowell. "My daughter will take care of your legal matters in the aftermath of your husband's death and the transplant. She specializes in criminal law, and will see you through the next few weeks. Once this is all behind you, she'll recommend someone who would be better for your day-to-day matters."

Melinda took out her card. "Call me anytime you need me. This may not go away for some time, and you will probably be called in again by the authorities. I'll be there whenever you're being questioned. And I'll also look over the legal papers."

And there would be questions, many of them.

As they were leaving Lowell handed a check to Melinda. "I want to give you another retainer to act as Gloria's attorney."

"Dad."

She looked at it. It was made out in the amount of five dollars. "Is that okay?"

She smiled. "That's fine."

Chapter Forty-six

Lowell entered Roland's office. The lieutenant was slugging down a cup of coffee, a grimace on his face. "Awful stuff," he said as Lowell sat.

"Want some?" asked the cop.

Lowell shook his head.

"Oh that's right," said Roland. "You never drink it after noon."

Lowell smiled. "There are some exceptions. But not today, thank you."

"What can I do for you, David?"

"I have some information that might be valuable."

Lowell told Roland about Williamson's almost confession to hiring McFarley to murder Karen's uncle. He also told him about the thumb drive and questionable genetic patents.

"What I know about genetics wouldn't fill a match book," said Roland. "I'll leave all that up to the DA's office. I catch killers and jaywalkers. Let someone else deal with the twenty-first century. So Williamson's dead. What a strange turn of events, wouldn't you say?"

Lowell shrugged. "It was an untimely death." He left out any mention of Gloria's role in his demise.

"Yes, but it seems quite fortunate for his son."

"Yes," said Lowell, "it did work out strangely balanced in some ways."

"You still have a problem on your hands, you know."

"McFarley." There was disgust in Lowell's voice.

Roland looked troubled. "McFarley is a tough case," he said, as he downed the last of his coffee. "We've had no luck finding him, and from what I can gather, he was very indebted to Williamson."

Lowell uncrossed his legs and stretched them out in front of him. Lately his right knee and hip had been giving him some trouble and he frequently needed to extend that leg out. "You didn't learn anything at the hospital?"

"No," Roland ran his hands through his hair. "Not much. Apparently Williamson saved his life years ago when he was badly cut up in a street brawl."

"That's when he got the scar on his face?"

"That's right," said Roland. "Williamson stitched him up and prevented him from bleeding to death. He didn't charge him. Ever since then McFarley has done favors for the good doctor. In fact, Williamson had scheduled plastic surgery to fix the scar."

Lowell nodded. "I guess that'll have to wait. So what now?"

The policeman leaned back in his chair. "Now you have to watch your back."

"For how long?"

The cop wasn't enjoying this at all. "I don't know."

"You know, Phil, I can't live in fear for the rest of my life."

"I know. But there's little else we can do. It could take years to catch him."

Lowell thought for a moment. "How devoted do you think McFarley was to Williamson?"

"No way of knowing. I suppose he felt some loyalty, though how much honor a professional killer and low life like him can have is a good topic for debate. You're gonna have to be careful until we can get him."

"And how about my extended family? If he's angry enough about the doctor's death, he may try to take it out on those closest to me."

Roland frowned. "It's a tough business you're in, as you know."

Lowell got up and walked to the window. Roland's office looked out over the busy side street. People were scurrying here and there, caught up in their own personal dramas. He turned to Roland.

"Phil, we've known each other for some time now. Have you ever wondered…"

"If it's all worthwhile?" asked the cop.

Lowell nodded.

"David, I chose this profession for a number of reasons. I like being an authority figure and I get a lot of pleasure out of helping others. And frankly, I'm not cut out for much else. This is what I'm good at. Also the pension and benefits are better than I could have gotten in private work. I'm not sure why you do it. You've obviously got more money than you need and could choose a different path."

"I suppose there are a number of reasons. Sarah has appointed herself my shrink. Maybe you should ask her." He laughed.

Roland smiled. "We'll keep the APB on for McFarley and I'll keep you posted if we hear anything."

Lowell got up to leave. "That's not good enough."

Roland nodded. "I didn't think it would be. Be careful, you've got a viper on your trail."

Lowell had his hand on the doorknob. He turned back to the policeman. "You can't live in fear."

"No," said Roland. "That's not living at all."

Lowell nodded to Roland, opened the door, and left.

Chapter Forty-seven

Lowell was at his desk looking over the day's trades when Sarah buzzed.

The door opened and Gloria entered. She seemed to walk a little taller and straighter.

Lowell stood. "Please sit down."

Her hands were still fidgety as she sat in the client's chair, but not as shaky. "I want to thank you for everything you did for me and my boys. It was a godsend that my husband found you."

"I'm very glad I could help. How is Edward?"

"He's doing okay. The doctors think he'll accept the new heart and be able to live a fairly normal life."

"What about you?"

"My nursing job ended. The old man died. And anyway, I have to find a job in my own name. It'll be difficult to explain the fifteen-year gap in my employment record. Right now I'm working at a local grocery store. The pay isn't much, and there are no benefits, but we'll get by." She stopped for a moment. "I don't know what I'm going to do about Edward's medicine. It's so expensive." A tear rode down her face. She brushed it away with a finger.

"Did you get health insurance?"

"Not yet. I'll try to get some kind of policy."

"I understand." He tugged on his ponytail. "Gloria, I have something for you."

She put a hand up. "I won't accept charity."

Lowell nodded and sat back in his chair. His admiration for this woman continued to grow. "I wouldn't offer it. Your husband gave me something to hold for you in case something unexpected happened."

She looked shocked. "He did?"

"It was actually for Edward, but now it's for your entire family."

"What could he have given you?"

"Well, you do know that he was a narcissist, what an astrologer would call a person with 1st house issues, who thought of his offspring as the living extension of himself."

She nodded. "I took courses in psychology in nursing school."

He bent down and picked up the brown leather briefcase Williamson had given him weeks before and placed it on the desk in front of her. "Your husband probably assumed there could be some difficulty in his scheme, although I doubt that he expected the results to be what they were. Still, he must have had some trepidation, because he had a contingency plan and left this with me when we first met."

She held the briefcase. "What is it?"

"Open it."

She clicked open the latches and sat staring at the crisp hundred-dollar bills. "Oh my God! How much money is this?"

"One million dollars."

She sat silently for a few moments still staring down at the money. Then she looked at Lowell. "I can't take this."

"You must. It's yours. There are several cases of fraud and theft being brought against your husband's estate. The justice department has frozen all of his assets and it will take years before anything will be accessible, if it ever is. He may very well have felt that discovery was imminent and put this aside to protect his son. This is the only legacy you are probably going to get from him, and you simply must accept it and use it to help raise your boys. You must think of them first. Edward's health bills will be enormous, even with insurance."

"But a million dollars! My God, what am I going to do with so much cash?"

"I suggest you get a safe deposit box and put most of it there. When you need money you'll go and get it. Some should be invested in an interest-bearing fund, but not enough to trigger an audit."

"You must take some."

Lowell waved his hand. "I've been handsomely rewarded in this case and I seek nothing more."

"I don't know what to say."

"I'm just glad it all worked out in the end. Do you have a bank account?"

She shook her head. "I was always too afraid he could track me so I never got one."

"I understand." He took out a card and handed it to her. "I want you to go see this man at the Chase branch over on Fifty-Third Street. The address is on the card. He's a friend of mine who will open an account for you and see to it that you have a safe deposit box set up immediately. It's all been arranged." He looked at his clock. "He's expecting you in about thirty minutes."

"I guess I'd better go grab a bus."

Lowell chuckled. "Under the circumstances I think it would be prudent to have my driver take you. He's waiting for you downstairs. I wouldn't want you to run around the city with a million dollars in cash. He'll also drive you back to Hartford when you're done."

She stood up and came around the desk and hugged Lowell. "I'll never forget you."

"Just keep in touch and let me know how the boys are doing."

"I will. You're a dear, sweet man and I can never repay you for what you have done for my family."

She took out a faded Polaroid picture of her holding Kevin and Edward. They couldn't have been more than a few days old. "I'd like you to have this, if you would. I only have a few pictures of our early life before…" she stopped.

Lowell took the snapshot. "This is incredibly generous, Gloria. I'll cherish it."

She smiled and left.

Chapter Forty-eight

Karen and Luigi showed up about noon. Sarah hadn't met Luigi yet and her giggles seeped through the door.

Karen knocked and entered Lowell's office. "We just wanted to say good-bye."

Luigi came around the desk and stood with his head in Lowell's lap. Lowell scratched the dog's ears as he talked.

"You've been great," she said. "I can't thank you enough. I've got the closure I needed on my uncle's death. At least now I know who was responsible. And why."

"Your uncle's actions forced Williamson's hand and led him to hire me. His work helped save those boys."

Karen nodded soberly. "I suppose there's some good in knowing that his death wasn't totally in vain, if it helped save someone else."

Lowell thought of Robert and the bodega owner and sighed. "Yes, there's some small comfort in that."

"If you're ever in L.A. and need a place, I've got that couch waiting for you. I know Luigi will be happy to see you."

She walked over to him, leaned over, and gave him an awkward hug. Luigi decided to get in on it and stood on his back legs. He licked Lowell's face a few times before Karen could get him down. Then she took Luigi's leash in hand, turned once with a small wave to Lowell, and headed for L.A.

◇◇◇

After Karen left, Sarah knocked and came in, walked across the room, and sat on the couch silently for a few moments. Then she stood up and actually huffed, audibly. She walked over to the window and shook her head.

Lowell turned in his swivel chair and watched her. "Something on your mind?"

She turned toward him, pushed her bright red hair back behind her ears, and frowned. "People stink."

Lowell half-smiled. "Is this news to you?"

"No. I'm not stupid. And I'm not a child. I know what the world is like."

"So, what's your problem?"

"I mean, what kind of a man would sacrifice one child for another?"

"Well, remember, in order to justify his actions, Williamson had convinced himself that Edward was more his son than Kevin. But that's an interesting question. What would you do if you were on a rowboat in the middle of the ocean and your spouse and your child were drowning and you could only save one? Which would it be?"

"That's not a fair question."

"Why not?"

"Because no matter which choice I made, I'd lose."

Lowell retied his ponytail. "Exactly. So what do you do?"

"Couldn't I jump in and save both and give up my own life?"

Lowell shook his head. "Sorry, not an option. The sharks are just about at the boat and you only have time to help one climb aboard. Do you save the love of your life, or your offspring? And what if you had two children drowning and must choose?"

She opened her mouth, but closed it without speaking.

"Have you ever read the book or seen the movie *Sophie's Choice?*"

Sarah shook her head.

"Rent it. Or better yet, read the book."

"What's it about?"

He smiled without joy. "It's about Sophie's choice. You'll understand."

"Okay, I'll pick it up. I usually like your reading suggestions."

"Good. Let me know what you think of it."

"I will."

She was quiet for a moment. "I think I might sign up for a class in aikido. What do you think?"

"I think that would be a wonderful idea." The detective leaned forward in his chair, a finger raised. "Just don't get cocky and get yourself into trouble."

"I won't. You made that point quite clearly. I just think it's one of the coolest things I've ever seen and I'd like to pursue it. Will you help me with it?"

"Anyway I can."

She smiled.

"Besides, it'll help you lose those few extra pounds you've been putting on."

"What!" Sarah turned around and looked at her derriere. "It's those damned marshmallows. They're addictive. But luckily they're almost all gone."

"Well," Lowell raised his eyebrows, "let's not order any more, okay?"

Sarah nodded and stood up. She headed for the door, then stopped and turned, a curious expression on her face.

"I'm sorry."

Lowell leaned back in his chair. "About what?"

"Robert."

Then she left.

Chapter Forty-nine

Lowell awoke at five and put on his usual garb of creased blue jeans, turtleneck, and loafers. He walked out of the townhouse on Ninety-Third Street, picked up the New York Times from his front stoop, and headed downtown toward his office. The sun was peaking across the horizon sending strange and colorful shadows across Manhattan Island. It was a beautiful late summer morning with just the slightest cool breeze brushing against his face.

He walked down Lexington Avenue past shuttered shops and quiet residential buildings. He seemed engrossed in his thoughts as he meandered across this tiny piece of land that had been his home for more than thirty years.

At Seventy-Ninth Street he turned left and went over toward the East River. He turned down York Avenue, still one of the most serene and gentle streets in the borough. He wondered how many of the residents in this neighborhood knew that this boulevard was named after Sergeant York, the pacifist who became a World War One hero and was portrayed by Gary Cooper in the movies.

He nodded to the occasional early riser he passed and the sleepy doormen, most of who had been on duty since before midnight and were awaiting their morning relief. Some nodded back. Others didn't seem inclined toward civility so late in their shift.

This area of York had many hospitals and medical schools, one after another. Ambulances passed him, even this early in the day. He walked passed Sloan Kettering with its many souls praying for a miracle. There was a single nurse outside preparing a wheelchair for some patient lucky enough to get to enjoy a bit of this wonderful sunny day.

Although caution was still called for, he wandered uninhibited and seemingly uncaring through the city streets. His attention was on his surroundings, and his manner was nonchalant and unhurried. He didn't seem to notice the man following him at a wide distance.

At Sixty-Fifth Street and York Avenue he stopped at a stone bench that was permanently secured to the building. He stretched like a house cat lying on the carpet as the morning sunshine streamed through a living room window. Then he sat on the bench.

The man following him stopped as well, about half a block behind. He crossed the street and hid behind a shuttered metal newsstand directly across the avenue from Lowell. He took out his revolver and screwed on a silencer.

Lowell sat back against the building unbothered and relaxed. He opened the newspaper, turned to the op-ed page, and began reading.

The gunman couldn't believe his luck. His prey was almost motionless as he balanced his gun hand against the edge of the kiosk, quietly took aim, and was about to fire.

"Drop it, scumbag," said a voice behind him. "I really don't want to have to kill you."

He turned suddenly to face Andy's gun aimed at his head. He stared Andy in the eye. At first it looked like he was about to turn the gun on him, but he realized the futility of it and dropped it onto the sidewalk.

Andy hit *send* on his cell phone. Lowell looked down at his phone and crossed the street. He approached Andy and the man.

"Well, McFarley," said Lowell, "looks like we've finally got you."

Chapter Fifty

The morning was bright and pleasantly warm. It wasn't really summer anymore, but autumn hadn't taken hold yet either. It was what many astrologers call *a cusp*—the transitional time between two periods.

Lowell went to the garage on Ninety-second Street. He'd called in advance and his car was waiting for him when he arrived. He gave the attendant a five dollar tip and got behind the wheel of the Volvo. He used to drive everywhere, often taking a day just to meander through Westchester or Long Island. But he had become complacent over the past eight years. Having Andy chauffeur him everywhere was often a blessing, but perhaps it had become a bit stifling. Every once in a while he needed to get out on his own.

He moved the seat back to a comfortable spot. Karen had pushed it too far forward when she had used it. Next he adjusted the rear view mirror, moved both side mirrors to accommodate him, and turned off the GPS. He knew where he was going.

Then he took a handful of CDs and loaded several into the player. He put the rest on the passenger's seat within easy reach. Although he had Sirius Radio in all of his vehicles, he sometimes wanted to hear his favorite recording artists and not leave it up to the DJs. Today he was in the mood for the blues.

He popped in a few CDs, including Muddy Waters, Eric Clapton, The Blues Project, and his favorite blues piano player,

Otis Spann. He hit the *random* button and the music started. "Otis in the Dark" was the first track. The steady rhythm of Spann's left hand made his body move in time with the beat.

He left the garage and went cross town to the Henry Hudson Parkway. Traffic was light and he was soon lost in that semiconscious state, driving on instinct. The trees were just starting to change, here and there a bright red next to a pale yellow. Autumn was always an emotional time for Lowell. Many significant events seem to happen in his life while the seasons were in flux, as if to remind us of how unstable are our best plans and how unsure is the future.

Time is a funny thing, he thought, as he drove unhurriedly. *Twenty years can go by in a flash. You jump from thirty-two to fifty-two with barely a realization, just the added aches and pains, and more frequent pit stops as the plumbing starts to rust. And just as suddenly those years will disappear and you feel like you're a kid again.*

He'd lived a long time already, more than half a century, and had seen such joy and sadness, the memories were humbling. *There's no way a person can be aware of it all the time. We keep blessedly busy so we don't always have to entertain our ghosts.* But Lowell knew his ghosts would be with him today, and he was ready to embrace them all.

The Blues Project was playing "Wake Me Shake Me." Al Kooper's somewhat wobbly vocals teetering atop his organ fills, Danny Kalb's incredibly fluid guitar licks, and Roy Blumenfeld's imaginative, rock-steady drums. Lowell smiled. He'd picked the right soundtrack for this journey.

The rhythm of the music and the soft, hypnotic rumbling of the road finally shook his mind free to meander uninhibited.

When he reached his destination, he got out of the car and stretched his legs. At first he zipped up his bombardier's jacket and turned the faux fur collar up around his neck. But it wasn't that cold yet; just a crisp bite to the air here in the foothills of the Catskills announcing that the new season had begun.

He unzipped the jacket and stood for a moment breathing in the fresh mountain air, gazing up at the trees, already much barer than downstate, but still a brilliant red or orange here and there. A multicolored carpet of leaves spread out before him on the dead-end road at the wood's edge, as it had so many times before. The memories threatened a flood of sensory input that he knew he could easily get lost within, and he had to push the past away so he could enjoy the unknown future. He took a step toward the house.

The front door opened and Catherine came out. She was wearing a very short blue dress and canary yellow shoes, just like she had the first time they'd made love at Freddie Finger's concert so many years before. She looked about nineteen.

When Lowell saw her, he stopped and gazed up into her bright, emerald, fearless eyes, looking for confirmation. He held his breath as she stood on the porch and looked at him for a few moments, trying to decide.

Then she winked.

To receive a free catalog of Poisoned Pen Press titles, please contact us in one of the following ways:

Phone: 1-800-421-3976
Facsimile: 1-480-949-1707
Email: info@poisonedpenpress.com
Website: www.poisonedpenpress.com

Poisoned Pen Press
6962 E. First Ave. Ste 103
Scottsdale, AZ 85251